MACPHERSON'S HIGHLAND FLING

Macpherson, the errand boy, often dreams about being a strong and brave hero, but really exciting things never seem to happen to him. Then a series of accidents lead to a surprise friendship, an unexpected holiday in the Highlands, and the chance for Macpherson to have some real-life adventures.

Scottish writer Lavinia Derwent has written many children's books. But of all her many characters she has the softest spot for Macpherson.

**Also by the same author,
and available in Knight Books**

Macpherson's Highland Fling

Lavinia Derwent

Illustrated by Lesley Smith

KNIGHT BOOKS
Hodder and Stoughton

Copyright © Lavinia Derwent 1980
Illustrations © Lesley Smith 1980

First published by Blackie & Son Ltd 1980

Knight Books edition 1982

British Library C.I.P.

Derwent, Lavinia
  Macpherson's highland fling.
  I. Title
  823'.914[F]   PZ7

  ISBN 0 340 28043 3

Printed and bound in Great Britain for
Hodder and Stoughton Paperbacks, a
division of Hodder and Stoughton Ltd.,
Mill Road, Dunton Green, Sevenoaks,
Kent (Editorial Office: 47 Bedford
Square, London, WC1 3DP) by
Cox & Wyman Ltd, Reading

Contents

1

A New Adventure

It was an exciting sound, the pipe band marching up the street to the rousing strains of *Scotland the Brave*. No wonder people cheered and clapped their hands. It was a sight worth seeing.

Every foot was in step, every kilt swayed in unison. They were big brawny fellows, all. Strong arms and sturdy legs. Especially the drum-major with the leopard-skin slung over his shoulders, the biggest and brawniest of them all. Proudly he marched, proudly he beat out the rhythm, proudly he tossed the drumsticks in the air, and deftly he caught them as they came down.

Big brawny fellows, all. Except one. Who was that little one at the rear in the skimpy kilt and with the message-basket over his arm?

It was Macpherson. He was marching proudest of the lot, though he was only the size of tuppence compared with the rest.

"Man, is it yourself, Macpherson?"

The Highland bobby, stopping the traffic to let the band through, stared at the message-boy in surprise.

"Ay, it's me."

Macpherson stuck out his chest under his shabby jersey. He could see himself in his imagination as the head of the regiment, even bigger and brawnier than the drum-major. Macpherson the Brave. He was the bravest of them all.

Not only that. He was a superman, Supreme Chief of Outer Space, a master magician with slaves at his command. It was amazing what imagination could do. He had only to snap his fingers and one of his slaves would appear.

"What is thy wish, O Master?"

"I wish thee to make the band go down past our flats — so that Grandpa can see."

He did not mention his Aunt Janet who also lived there, for she would be away out working, and was not interested in noisy bands. But Grandpa, even if he was busy making ships-in-bottles, always had time to take a look out of the window. *He* liked the same things as Macpherson.

"Ay, we're a fine pair, Macpherson my hearty!"

That's what they were; a pair. Macpherson

always wanted to share everything with Grandpa. What was the use of being head of the regiment if Grandpa could not admire him?

Boom-boom-boom! The pipes played faster and faster, the drummer beat the time louder and louder.

Perhaps they would cross the big bridge over the river Clyde. Then they could go past the place where the princess lived. Not a real princess, but she lived like one in a fine house with her uncle, Sir George.

He had met Annabelle — the princess — when he rescued the Tiger-Cat. It had been a poor lost stray, but now Annabelle had given it a home. Lucky Tiger-Cat!

"Mac-pher-thon!"

A shrill lisping voice could be heard above the music, and little Maisie Murphy came hurrying after him, staggering in her big boots which were hand-me-downs from an older member of the large Murphy family. No mistaking Maisie for a princess. Her stockings were hanging down, her hair was tousled, and she wore a mixty-maxty set of garments which might have come out of a rag-bag. But her rosy face was shining with excitement, as she hurried to catch up with Macpherson.

"Wait for me, Macpherthon. Ithn't thith fun?"

Yes, it was fun, but it was a man's job. Macpherson did not like the thought of a lassie following him.

"You'd better go home, Maisie," he said firmly. "Home!" he repeated.

Maisie's lip began to tremble. Soon the tears would be rolling down her cheeks. She was a great one for laughing one minute and crying the next.

Macpherson looked alarmed. It would never do if she burst into tears in front of the regiment. She looked so pathetic that his heart began to soften, and he fumbled in his pocket for something that he knew would cheer her up. A sweet. It was a caramel which he had been saving up for Grandpa.

"There!" he said, thrusting it at her.

"Oh thankth, Macpherthon. You're great."

"Yes, so I am," agreed Macpherson.

Maisie brushed away her tears, tore off the paper and soon was sucking happily at the caramel. But she still followed him, swinging her tattered skirt and lifting her feet high in the air, trying to keep in step with the music.

Macpherson took her firmly by the hand and guided her on to the pavement. The band was passing the park gates by now and people were crowding round to watch. But it spoiled the look of things to have Maisie trotting alongside, trying to thrust her grubby little hand in his. So Macpherson was determined to get rid of her.

"Why not go into the park and play on the swings?" he suggested. He knew this was one of her favourite ploys.

"Yeth I will, if you'll come, too, Macpher-thon."

"No, no! Not just now."

Maisie hesitated. "Will you come later, Macpherthon?"

"I'll see."

Macpherson did not like to tell lies — not direct ones. He had no intention of playing on the swings, but how else could he get rid of Maisie?

"Righto! I'll thee you later, Macpherthon."

She let go his hand and he marched off, while she stood waiting, hoping he would turn and wave to her. But he was too busy tossing his empty message-basket up into the air, pre-tending to be the drum-major.

Once more he called up his imaginary slaves. "I wish thee to turn to the right."

The band turned to the left instead. Wasn't

11

it like the thing? "Och well!" said Macpherson to himself, catching the basket as it came down. "It can't be helped." But the trouble about turning to the left was that he would have to go past the grocer's shop where he worked: W. McGLASHAN, FAMILY GROCER, established 1900. *If* he could get past without being seen.

There was someone at the door, but it was only Miss Peacock, the assistant, and she was all right. She had a soft spot for Macpherson, as he had for her. Not like Mr McGlashan. Old Skinflint, everyone called him. He had no soft spots for anyone. Mr McGlashan hated everything except money. Message-boys most of all, and Macpherson in particular.

But Miss Peacock was a gem. She sometimes gave him some biscuits to take home to Grandpa, and she always stood up for him against Old Skinflint.

Macpherson held his head high and tried to make himself look bigger so that she would admire him as he marched past.

"Hi, Macpherson!"

She had seen him. Miss Peacock gave him a wave and tapped her feet in time to the music, as if she was marching, too. Macpherson tossed the basket higher into the air. It was a great feeling, catching it as it came down.

But his hour of glory was soon at an end. Someone else had come to the door, but not to watch the band. What did he care for the big drum? Old Skinflint was more interested in his best customer whom he was ushering out with great ceremony and false smiles.

"*Good*bye, Mrs Macfarlane-Brown, and thank you for calling. It's always a pleasure to see *you*. Yes! I'll be sure to send your order with the message-boy."

The message-boy! That's what Macpherson was. Not the head of the regiment, not a superman, not Chief of Outer Space, nor a master magician with slaves at his command. He was only a ragamuffin with not even a caramel left in his pocket.

His step faltered and he lost some of his swagger. But he still stuck to his imagination. Maybe Old Skinflint had not seen him. Maybe he could slink into the shop without being noticed. Maybe . . .

But Mr McGlashan had eyes in the back of his head. No sooner had he bowed Mrs Macfarlane-Brown into her car than the false smiles left his face and he came rampaging into the shop, looking like thunder.

"And what do *you* think you were up to?" he

demanded, catching Macpherson by the scruff of the neck. "Behaving like an idiot! Throwing my good message-basket about! Dilly-dallying in the street, following the band in *my* time. Message-boys! They're perfect pests! I'll flay you alive, that's what I'll do. How dare you?"

"Please, Mr McGlashan sir, I'm very sorry."

"Sorry! I'll make you sorry!" Old Skinflint was working himself up into one of his red-hot tempers, shaking Macpherson till his backbone rattled. "I'm warning you! Any

more nonsense and I'll chop you into little pieces. Message-boys!"

Miss Peacock gave a cough in the background to distract his attention. "About the order, Mr McGlashan. Do you want it made up now?"

"The order? Made up now? Yes, of course; the sooner the better."

He gave Macpherson a final shake and thrust him aside. Business came first.

For a time he concentrated on the order, helping Miss Peacock to collect the goods from the shelves and pile them up in a heap on the counter. There were so many that she was almost hidden behind them.

"Mercy!" she gasped, adding a tin of peaches to the pile. "Mrs Macfarlane-Brown's surely laying in a big store."

"She's entertaining the Lord Provost," said the grocer, ticking off another item from the list.

"The Lord Provost!" gasped Macpherson. "Jings!"

The Lord Provost was a VIP, the Most Important Person in the whole city of Glasgow. And what was more, Macpherson knew him. He was Sir George Stuart, Annabelle's uncle, and he lived in a great big mansion house called The

Grange, Pollok Road, Glasgow, Scotland, The World. Macpherson had been there, visiting Annabelle and the Tiger-Cat. But, of course, the grocer did not know that.

"The boy'll never carry all that lot, poor soul," said Miss Peacock, giving Macpherson a sympathetic look over the mound of groceries.

"Two dozen eggs," said Old Skinflint, ticking off the last item. "He'll have to take them in a taxi. Mrs Macfarlane-Brown's in a hurry for them. And see that the eggs don't get shoogled," he added, giving Macpherson another shake to drive home his point.

"Oh no, Mr McGlashan, sir, I won't shoogle them. I'll be as careful as can be," promised Macpherson.

His eyes were shining. A taxi! Fancy that!

Old Skinflint whistled one up, and then packed all the goods inside. Except the eggs. He put *them* in a special basket and handed it to Macpherson. "Here, you! You'd better sit beside the driver. And see that those eggs don't get . . ."

"Shoogled!" Macpherson grinned at him and settled down beside the driver, with the basket held carefully on his knee. "I'll watch them, sir. Cheerio, Miss Peacock! Cheerio, Mr Skin . . . Mr McGlashan, sir! Drive on!"

Macpherson, feeling like the Lord Provost himself, set off on his first taxi-ride.

The driver was a silent man. He had other things to do than talk to a message-boy. If he wasn't changing gear or hooting his horn, he was listening to the messages coming in from headquarters. "Car wanted at Number 10, Kelvinside Avenue." "Anyone near Canal Street?" "Car wanted . . . "

"Would you mind going a wee bit slower?" asked Macpherson suddenly. "I want to wave to somebody."

When they reached the big crossing, Macpherson saluted the Highland bobby.

"Man! Is it yourself, Macpherson?"

"Ay, it's me."

Macpherson, chief citizen of Glasgow, riding around in his private taxi.

CRASH!

Macpherson had no idea how it happened. All he knew was that he was pitchforked on to the pavement in company with two dozen broken eggs, while pounds of butter, tins of peaches and goodness knows what else went rolling into the gutter. He was not troubled about whether he had broken any bones. It was the eggs that worried him.

"Oh jings!" he gasped, as the yolks went

trickling along the pavement. "What'll Old Skinflint say?"

2

In the Soup

A large shaggy animal was leaning over him, sniffling into his ears and licking his face in a friendly fashion. Macpherson snuggled against him, glad to have support of any kind.

It was a dog, but such a dog as Macpherson had never seen before. Bigger, tougher-looking and yet gentler than any he had ever known.

"Good boy!" said Macpherson, leaning against the comforting creature. "Nice dog!"

"*Rusty!*"

A shout came from the distance, followed by a piercing whistle.

The dog cocked his ears as his master came hurrying across the road. He was big and shaggy, too. Tough-looking yet gentle. What was more, he was wearing something strange over his shoulders. Goodness gracious! It was a leopard-skin.

"Jings!" gasped Macpherson, gazing up at him. "You're the drum-major."

"Ay, that's me," said the big man in a loud rumbly voice, as if he was used to shouting into the far distance. "And what might you be doing sitting on the pavement among all them broken eggs?"

"Oh help!" said Macpherson, looking at the egg-shells in dismay. "I'm in the soup! Mr McGlashan'll skin me alive, and so will Mrs Macfarlane-Brown. You see, I was in a taxi . . ."

That was as far as he got before the hullaballoo broke out. Macpherson continued to sit on the pavement leaning against Rusty, while the taxi-driver, the drum-major and the Highland bobby all went at it hammer-and-tongs over his head. They were all speaking at once, and it was difficult to sort out who was saying what, but one thing was certain. They were all angry!

"It was *his* fault," raged the taxi-driver. "That man with the muckle dog. I had to swerve to avoid it and went slap-bang into the lamp-post."

"Slap-bang's the word!" roared the drum-major. "I saw you. You were going far too fast."

"Nothing of the sort! If you'd look after your muckle dog . . . I've a good mind to bash your head off."

"Bash away!" cried the big man, flexing his muscles. "I'm ready for you."

"Now, now," said the Highland bobby, getting out his notebook. "Names and addresses, please." He turned to the drum-major. "You first, Hamish."

It was obvious he knew the big man. No doubt they both came from the Highlands, perhaps from the same village. However, names and addresses had to be given. Even Macpherson had to give his address, though the policeman knew fine where he lived.

"Are you all right, Macpherson?" asked the bobby, licking his pencil.

"Ay, I'm okay. Except for the eggs."

"Och! Never heed the eggs."

Never heed the eggs! It was all right for the Highland bobby. He didn't work for Old Skinflint. And what about Mrs Macfarlane-Brown and the Lord Provost?

Macpherson had often been in the soup before, but never in such hot soup as this. He doubted if he would live to tell the tale to Grandpa.

They had come to some sort of truce by now, the three men. They were all walking round the taxi, kicking it here and there to see if there was any damage done, opening the doors and dusting out the loose sugar and tea that was strewn all over the floor.

"Such a mess!" moaned the taxi-driver. "It's worse than confetti."

"You'll get compensation," promised the bobby. "And as for you, Macpherson, I'm thinking we'd better come with you and explain matters to Mr McGlashan."

It took some explaining! Old Skinflint was all for skinning Macpherson alive without listening to any explanations.

"That message-boy! He's a perfect pest. I might have known he'd make a mess of things. I *told* him not to shoogle the eggs. I *warned* him to be careful. And all my good groceries ruined! Skinning him alive is too good for him."

"Now, now, Mr McGlashan," soothed the bobby. "The boy couldn't help it. Anybody can get involved in an accident."

But the grocer was not convinced. "How is it that something always happens to *him*? Answer me that!" He glared at Macpherson and at the dented tins and broken biscuits they had rescued from the wreck. "And what about Mrs Macfarlane-Brown's order? And her expecting the Lord Provost."

"The Lord Provost, is it?" said the drum-major, coming forward with his great dog at his heels. "That'll be Sir George Stuart of The Grange?"

"Take that dog out of the shop," ordered Old Skinflint. "I can't stand beasts."

It was obvious that the big man couldn't stand *him* either. But he obediently took the dog to the door and said, "Sit, Rusty!" in a commanding voice. Then he came back, as cool as could be, and addressed himself to Miss Peacock instead of the grocer.

"As I was saying about the Lord Provost..."

"That's right. It's Sir George," said Miss Peacock, looking admiringly at the man's kilt and the leopard-skin over his shoulder. Then she added, as a dig at her employer, "He's a friend of Macpherson."

"Well, now!" The big man (Hamish McTavish was the name he had given the bobby to put in his notebook) turned to Macpherson and gripped him by the hand. Such a grip! Macpherson thought all his bones were crushed. Yet it was such a friendly grip that he tried not to wince at the pain.

"Greetings to you, Macpherson! He's a friend of mine, too, and so is Miss Annabelle. They sometimes come and stay in the Big House at Glen Bogle where I live. Away beyond Oban, it is. Sir George is the laird in those parts. Owns a lot of the land, and often comes for the fishing and the Highland Games."

"Mercy me!" said Macpherson, staring at him. "Isn't it a wee small world?"

Old Skinflint did not care about the wee small world or about Glen Bogle or the fishing or the Highland Games. "What about Mrs Macfarlane-Brown's order?" he demanded. "And all the groceries ruined?"

"You'll get compensation," the bobby promised him as he had promised the taxi-driver. "You'd better make the order up again. I'll see that it gets delivered and explain matters to the customer."

"I'll come with you, Fergus," said the big man. Fergus! So *that* was the Highland bobby's name. Macpherson was learning things. "Macpherson'll be none the worse for an extra bodyguard."

He gave one wink at the message-boy and another at Miss Peacock who was busy piling up a new mound of groceries. Then he wandered outside to wait beside his dog, out of the way of Old Skinflint who was rattling tins off the shelves and dumping them angrily on the counter.

"Message-boys!" he kept muttering to himself. "Perfect pests! They should all be shot."

It was not a taxi they took this time. It was a police car! Imagine! Macpherson could scarcely believe his luck. What an amazing world this was. Anything could happen.

It was a tight squash before they all got settled in, Hamish and the Highland bobby in the back along with the groceries, and Macpherson and the dog in front along with the driver. But this time there was no basket of eggs on his knee.

"*You*'d better take them," growled Old Skinflint thrusting the basket at the bobby. "Can't trust that boy. And mind *you* don't shoogle them."

"I'll mind," grinned the bobby as if *he* was the message-boy. "They'll get there safe enough. Barring accidents!"

Macpherson enjoyed his ride, with Rusty snuggling at his feet and music coming from the radio. He had expected to hear messages, like the ones in the taxi but more exciting. "Desperate criminal at large . . ." "Smash-and-grab at the Royal Bank . . ." "Send the Flying Squad . . ."

But not a word! Nothing except music. *Scotland the Brave*!

"That's *your* tune, isn't it, Mr Hamish, sir?" said Macpherson, turning round and speaking to the drum-major.

"That's it, Macpherson. A fine tune. Fairly stirs the blood."

"Mind the eggs!" warned the bobby as the big man began to swing an imaginary drumstick in the air in time to the music. "Man, Hamish, you haven't improved any."

"Och! Who wants to improve?" Hamish gave one of his great laughs and leaned over to Macpherson. "Let's hear all about it."

"All about what, Mr Hamish, sir?" asked Macpherson over his shoulder.

"All about you, of course."

"Me?" said Macpherson, surprised. "There's nothing to tell."

"Nothing!" scoffed the bobby, holding the basket of eggs steady on his knees. "Man, Macpherson, what about all your adventures? They'd fill a book."

"Och well," said Macpherson, trying to look modest. And he began to tell about his adventures. The real ones, not the imaginary kind. *They* would fill dozens of books. But the real ones were exciting enough. He told about saving Maisie Murphy when she fell into the canal, about Grandpa and Aunt Janet, and about how he met Sir George, the Lord Provost. There were still heaps of other things to tell when the car came to a stop outside Mrs Macfarlane-Brown's door.

"To be continued," grinned the big man, hitching up his leopard-skin. "How would you like to come up to Glen Bogle, Macpherson, and have some more adventures in the Highlands?"

"Me?" gasped Macpherson, dumbfounded.

"Ay, you! You could come for your holidays and help me in the croft and go out with the fishing-boats and take part in the Highland Games," said the drum-major, as if it was all settled. "Rusty would like it fine. He seems to have taken a fancy to you."

The big dog rubbed his shaggy coat against Macpherson's legs as if to say, "Come on, Macpherson. Come to the Highlands."

It was such a new and splendid idea that Macpherson just stood on the pavement and gaped up at the drum-major. He had been in the Highlands often enough in his imagination, amongst the heathery hills and the lochs. He could see himself out with the fishing-boats and winning trophies at the Highland Games. Macpherson the Great, chieftain of the clan. But, of course, it was only a daydream.

"What are you standing there gaping for? Bring the groceries in at once and stop wasting time."

Mrs Macfarlane-Brown was calling to them from the doorstep, her face flushed with anger.

"I've been waiting for ages. Mr McGlashan rang up to say there was some delay. Some delay, indeed! My visitors will be here any moment. It's really too bad. That message-boy . . .!"

"It wasn't the boy's fault."

Again the Highland bobby stepped in to make the peace, handing over the basket of eggs, as careful as could be, while the big man helped to carry the groceries up the steps. But Mrs Macfarlane-Brown, like the grocer, was determined to put the blame on Macpherson.

"You!" she raged at him. "You're always getting into mischief. I've a good mind to change my grocer. I've told Mr McGlashan . . . Oh dear! Here's the Lord Provost's car and me not half ready . . ."

She hurried away inside while the great car came gliding to a standstill. Smithers, the chauffeur, stepped out to open the door, splendid in his uniform. He grinned at Macpherson and said out of the corner of his mouth, " 'Allo, Macpherson. 'Ow are yer, chum?" He and Macpherson had met and made friends in the past.

"I'm fine, Mr Smithers, sir."

And now someone else spoke to Macpherson. "Hullo, boy."

It was the great man himself. The Lord Provost, stepping from the car and shaking the message-boy warmly by the hand. "We haven't seen you at The Grange for a while. Annabelle was wondering when you were coming to see her and the Tiger-Cat."

"Och, I'll be coming soon, Sir George, sir," said Macpherson, flushing with pleasure and hoping that Mrs Macfarlane-Brown was watching from the window.

"Hamish! It's yourself!"

Sir George had caught sight of the drum-major and was slapping him on the back, leopard-skin and all. "How's everything at Glen Bogle? I'll be coming up soon for the fishing."

"And very welcome you'll be, Sir George."

Macpherson would have liked to stay there listening to them, but he had to run backwards and forwards with the groceries. The men were talking about *him*. He could tell that by the way they kept looking at him, and he could hear Sir George saying, "By jove! A splendid idea. He can come up with us in the car. Plenty of room, and he'll be company for Annabelle. A splendid idea!''

A splendid idea! Macpherson tried to control himself from turning a somersault there and then on the doorstep. But in the end it got the better of him. He *had* to do it. His

head went down, his legs went up, and Mrs Macfarlane-Brown, coming out to receive the Lord Provost, gave a horrified shriek.

"That message-boy! Turning somersaults on my doorstep! I'll complain to Mr McGlashan, that's what I'll do. I never knew such behaviour. Message-boys! They're worse than wild animals."

3

The Search-Party

"Heave-ho, my hearty! Come on, Macpherson! Tell me everything."

Grandpa beamed at Macpherson and Macpherson beamed back at Grandpa. This was the time of day they both liked best, when Aunt Janet had gone off to bed and they had the shabby kitchen to themselves.

"It's high time you were both bedded," she had scolded before yawning her way to her own dark little bedroom. "You'll not be so bright in the morning, the pair of you."

She said the same thing every night, and Grandpa always gave the same reply. "We'll get bedded in two-three minutes, and we'll be brighter than bees in the morning. Away you go, Janet woman. Goodnight, sleep tight, don't let the bugs bite."

When the coast was clear he put aside the model ship on which he had been working, drew his chair closer to Macpherson and gave all his attention to the boy. "Come on,

Captain. Tell me every single thing."

First, Macpherson took a chocolate biscuit covered with silver paper from his pocket and handed it solemnly to the old man. "With Miss Peacock's compliments, and can I have the silver paper for my collection, please, Grandpa?"

"Splice the mainbrace!" The old man smacked his lips and wagged his beard. "Tell Miss Peacock from me she's a gem. A real gem! Will you have half, Macpherson?"

"No, I'm not hungry," said Macpherson, averting his gaze. He knew how much the old man liked sweet things and especially chocolate biscuits. "You eat it, Grandpa; it'll do you good."

"Just a mouthful, to please me," said Grandpa, breaking off a generous portion and passing it across the table. "Now then, Macpherson, begin at the beginning."

Between munches Macpherson told his story, as he told all his adventures to the old man. It was almost better than the adventures themselves, this re-telling of them to Grandpa who was the best audience in the world and wanted to know every single little detail.

"What did you say his name was, the big fella with the leopard-skin?"

"Hamish McTavish of Glen Bogle." Macpherson rolled out the words in a big mouthful.

"Man! I like the sound of *him*. He'll likely be a great hand at tossing the caber."

"What's that, Grandpa?"

"The caber? Och! It's a great muckle thing like a telegraph-pole. It takes a big fella to handle it, like your Mr Hamish McTavish of Glen Bogle. But you'll likely be seeing it yourself, Macpherson, at the Highland Games."

Macpherson's eyes were shining like stars. "Do you *really* think I could go, Grandpa?"

"Why not, my old shipmate?" Grandpa swallowed the last of his chocolate biscuit. He had been spinning it out as long as he could, but all good things come to an end. "Miracles can happen."

That was another thing Grandpa and Macpherson had in common. They both believed in miracles.

"Whoopee!"

Macpherson restrained himself in time from getting up and turning a somersault. If he made too much noise Aunt Janet would come through and tell them it was high time they were bedded. And besides, he remembered what had happened on Mrs Macfarlane-Brown's doorstep. That was another thing he had to tell Grandpa.

He was in the midst of the story when they heard footsteps outside the door, followed by a shrill ring at the doorbell.

"Ship ahoy!" cried Grandpa. "Who's that?"

"Goodness gracious!" said Macpherson, staring at the door. "It could be *anybody*." His imagination ran away with him. "Maybe it's the Queen."

The old man chuckled. "Och ay! That's who it'll be. She'll have come to knight you. *Arise, Sir Macpherson!*"

"No, no; it'll be *you*, Grandpa," said Macpherson, nobly giving the honour to the old man. "*Arise, Sir Grandpa!*"

A louder, shriller ring at the doorbell.

"Maybe it's yon big fella from Glen Bogle," said Grandpa, trying to get up on his stiff legs.

"Sit still, Grandpa. I'll go."

Nobody could have looked less like the Queen or less like big Hamish McTavish of Glen Bogle than the little man who stood, panting, on the doorstep. It was Mr Murphy who lived down below, untidy and unshaven as usual, but with an unusual look of anxiety on his face. Like all the large family of Murphies, he took life as it came and was seldom up or down.

But tonight something had happened to upset him.

"Begob! And is she not here?" he said in his rich Irish tongue, peering past Macpherson into the kitchen. "She's after getting herself proper lost this time, that one."

"Lost!" said Macpherson. "What one?"

"Bedad! And it's herself. Maisie Murphy. Not a sight or a sound of her have we had all day. And the missis nearly out of her mind." He leaned wearily against the door.

"Come in, Murphy man. Sit down and rest yourself," said Grandpa kindly.

"Rest meself, is it?" The little man shook his head. "With me daughter lying dead as a doornail. Run over by a bus, maybe. Or drownded in the river Clyde . . ."

Macpherson went as white as a sheet. Wee Maisie Murphy run over by a bus! Wee Maisie Murphy drownded in the River Clyde!

"Wh-When did you see her last?" he asked her father.

"Shure, it was this morning, as ever was, and her running away after the pipe band."

"Oh, jings!"

Macpherson suddenly remembered. He clapped his hand to his mouth and turned even whiter. "I sort of half-promised her . . ."

"Macpherson!" said Grandpa, reproachfully. He was always on the boy's side, but deceit and lies he could not abide. "You broke your promise?"

Macpherson looked miserable. Apart from being worried about Maisie, he hated to be out of favour with the old man. "It wasn't a real promise, Grandpa. I only said I might."

"Might what?" cried Murphy, impatiently. "Speak up, me boyo! Is it about me daughter?"

Macpherson nodded unhappily. "Well, you see, it was like this." And he told how he had sent Maisie away to the park with the half-promise that he would join her later, on the swings.

"Bedad! She'll still be there. Locked in, as like as not!" cried Murphy, turning to go.

"Wait!" said Macpherson. "I'll come with you."

"Yes, you do that, Macpherson," said Grandpa gravely. "And remember, promises should be kept."

"I'll remember, Grandpa," said Macpherson solemnly.

"What's going on out there?" called Aunt

Janet from the bedroom. "Macpherson, it's high time you were bedded."

But Macpherson was running after Murphy, out into the strange dark streets with all his happy thoughts of the Highlands forgotten. He could think of nothing now except Maisie Murphy and his broken promise. "I'll thee you later, Macpherthon," she had said. And he hadn't turned up. If any harm had come to Maisie, he could never forgive himself, never!

In desperation he summoned up one of his imaginary slaves.

"What is thy wish, O Master?"

"I wish thee to let us find Maisie safe and sound, and the sooner the better."

But first they had to find the park keeper, and a fine job they had knocking him up out of his bed.

"What's going on? What do you want at this time of night?" he roared from his bedroom window.

"The keys, please," said Macpherson in an urgent voice.

"Keys! Fiddlesticks! Away you go and let me get back to my bed."

"It's an *emergency!*" called Macpherson.

Emergency or no, they had to get a policeman before the park keeper would come with the keys. It was not the Highland bobby — he had gone off duty — but a young fellow who was new to the job and glad of an excuse to liven up a dull night's work.

"Burglars, is it?" he said with a gleam in his eye, hoping for a new stripe.

"No, no! It's wee Maisie Murphy," explained Macpherson. "I think she's got locked in the park."

"A wee lassie!" It was a great come-down from a burglar. Still, it was better than nothing. "Right! Let's get on with it," said he, taking charge.

It was eerie prowling about in the park at night. Not the familiar daytime park, but quite a different place in the dark, with all the flowers folded in their beds sound asleep, and strange whispers from the bushes as the wind rustled their leaves.

"Begob! I've got the shivers in me back," said Murphy, moving closer to the policeman.

The lake was deserted, with the ducks crouching by the reeds at the side, letting out sleepy quacks now and again. An aeroplane throbbed high overhead, winging its way to the unknown like a migrating bird. A town clock chimed in the distance.

But no sign of wee Maisie Murphy.

"Would she have fallen into the lake, maybe?" suggested the policeman in a matter-of-fact voice, as if it made no difference one way or another.

"What?" cried Macpherson, aghast at the thought. He ran helter-skelter round the lake calling, "Maisie! Maisie!" startling the ducks and almost tumbling in himself. "Are you there, Maisie?"

He peered at the glinting water, his heart turning over with fear in case he should see her face floating on the surface amongst the water lilies. But no! Thank goodness! He could see nothing but the faint reflection of the moon.

The men were searching under the bushes, pulling back the branches and disturbing the sleeping creatures underneath. A rabbit sprang out and went scampering away.

"I'll get *you* in the morning," said the park keeper grimly. "Let's turn it in. There's no use looking any further."

"No, no!" cried Macpherson in distress. "She's here somewhere. I'm certain sure."

"Fiddlesticks!" said the keeper crossly. "How can you be certain sure?"

"I've got a feeling in my bones," insisted

Macpherson. "Let's have one more look. Please!"

"Oh, all right! Just five minutes. I'm not going to hang about in the park all night. I get enough of it through the day."

He went grumbling away to join Murphy and the policeman, still peering under the bushes. But Macpherson looked up at the sky instead. He had one special star there. Yes! There it was twinkling just for him. Perhaps it could help him now.

"What is thy wish, O Great Macpherson, Lord of Outer Space?"

"I wish thee to find wee Maisie Murphy."

The magic worked! The star went in and out, out and in, as if sending a signal. And it was the moon that received the message, for suddenly it sailed out from behind a cloud and directed its beams on the glass-covered greenhouses.

Macpherson let out a shout that went echoing through the empty park.

"Begob! And have you found her, me boyo?" called Murphy, running across the grass and knocking over the KEEP OFF sign.

"No, but I know where she is," said Macpherson confidently. He pointed to the greenhouses, glinting in the moonlight.

"Well now, it's a possibility," admitted the keeper. "I *could* have locked her in."

He had!

They found her asleep in a corner, curled up like a kitten, almost suffocated with the heavy scent of exotic flowers.

"Macpherthon," she murmured as they shook her gently to waken her up. "You've come at latht. I waited ever tho long at the thwingth."

"Yes, I know. I'm sorry, Maisie," said Macpherson, so thankful to have found her that it seemed as if a heavy burden had rolled off his shoulders. "Are you okay?"

She smiled sleepily and clutched his hand. "Yeth, I'm okay, now that you're here, Macpherthon."

"Come on, me darlin'," said her father, hoisting her up. "I'll carry you home to bed."

"No, no, I want Macpherthon."

She was a solid little bundle, far too heavy for him, but Macpherson stuck it out. It was the least he could do after breaking his promise.

"Thankth, Macpherthon, thith ith better than being on the thwingth," she said drowsily, and once more drifted off into dreamland.

Macpherson hoisted up his burden and continued happily on his way. All was well. He could now look Grandpa in the face again.

4

Macpherson in Peril

"Hi! Rusty! Wait for me!"

Macpherson, running after the shaggy
sheepdog, quickened his pace as Rusty went
bounding away in front of him up the heathery
hillside overlooking the sea.

The dog had an object in view. A stray
sheep had wandered on to a ledge and might
tumble down the cliff if it took a wrong step.
But the boy had no object. Except the joy of
being in the open air, with the sea splashing on
the rocks and the freedom of Glen Bogle for a
whole wonderful fortnight.

The miracle had happened.

He was here, staying in the whitewashed
cottage down below with Hamish McTavish
(Big Hamish he was called here) a hundred
miles and more away from the bustle of the big
city and from the scoldings of Old Skinflint.

In the distance he could see the towers and
turrets of the Big House where Sir George and
Annabelle were staying. It was more than a

big house — it was a castle with an old drawbridge and ramparts. And a ghost! Lady Annabelle Stuart, it was, who had been a friend of Bonnie Prince Charlie himself.

Annabelle had seen her once, wandering in the moonlight, and Macpherson was determined to see her, too. He wanted to see every single thing in Glen Bogle, even ghosts. Monsters, too, if there were any.

"Oh look!" he cried, speaking to himself since there was no one else there, and pointing high overhead. "See that great muckle bird."

It was something else he was seeing for the first time. An eagle hovering high up near its eyrie. Big Hamish had told him about it. He was as good as an encyclopedia. Big Hamish knew everything. He was almost as good as Grandpa.

Macpherson's foot faltered on the heather as he thought of Grandpa and saw him in his mind's eye, sitting at the window peering out at the ships on the river Clyde, back home in Glasgow. The holiday was great. The only sad thing was saying goodbye to Grandpa, even though it was only for a fortnight. They had never been parted for so long before.

The old man had put on a great show of

cheerfulness as if he was glad Macpherson was leaving.

"Heave-ho, my hearty!" he had cried, gripping Macpherson's hand when it came to the final parting and leaving a whole fifty pence piece in it. "You'll write?"

"Yes, Grandpa, I'll write," gulped Macpherson, staring at the money. "Can you spare it, Grandpa?"

"A millionaire like me! Of course, I can spare it. I sold one of my ships-in-bottles the other day. Rolling in money, that's me! Put it in your pocket, my old shipmate."

But Macpherson had noticed that the old man's pipe was empty. Just wait till *he* was a millionaire. Grandpa would have the biggest pipe in the world and the best tobacco to go with it. And cigars as well. Great muckle big ones, even longer than Sir George's.

At the thought of Sir George he suddenly came back to earth and Glen Bogle, pushing aside the memory of the final goodbyes and of Maisie Murphy's trembling lip as she pleaded, "Pleathe let me come, too, Macpherthon. *Pleathe!*"

A sharp yelp from Rusty. Something was wrong. The big dog seemed to be trying to attract Macpherson's attention as if he was shouting, "SOS! Come on, Macpherson! I need your help."

The boy wasted no time in answering the call. He took to his heels and went helter-skeltering up the steep hill, arriving at the cliff-side out of breath.

Yes! Rusty needed help right enough and so did the sheep. Silly thing! She had backed half-way over the cliff and was stuck in such a position that she could not heave herself forward. She could move backwards all right but that would lead her to her doom. One false step and she would go tumbling head-over-tail on to the rocks and into the swirling sea.

That would be a terrible thing to happen. Not only for the sheep but for Big Hamish whose flock was so small that he needed every single one to help him pay his way. It was up to Macpherson to prevent such a disaster.

"Come on, Macpherson. Do something," he told himself.

The dog sat watching, his tongue hanging out, looking up at the boy as if to say, "Now you're here, Macpherson, I'll leave it to you."

At the right moment Macpherson had an inspiration. "That's what I'll do," he decided. "Go down below and *push* her up."

Rusty seemed to understand and approve.

He sat still, fixing the sheep with his eye as if daring her to move. Macpherson knew what the dog was doing. Big Hamish had told him about it. All good sheepdogs have this strange power. The power of the eye. They can fix a sheep to the spot if they want her to stay still. Mesmerism, that's what Big Hamish called it. Right enough, he knew everything. As long as Rusty used this power of mesmerism on the sheep she would stay still.

But there was no staying still for Macpherson. Action was what counted. He went down the hill a little way and peered over the cliff to see how he could manage it. Goodness! How steep it was and how easy it would be to go head-first on to the jagged rocks. But he had better not look down.

Macpherson went over the edge carefully, clinging with his hands to a strong clump of heather. His foot slipped, then came to rest on a ledge. If he crept along sideways like a crab he could reach the right spot just underneath the stranded sheep.

"Come on, Macpherson!" he urged himself.

He took a deep breath and started on his dangerous mission. It was like walking a tight-rope, the same as a circus performer, with the hungry sea waiting below to swallow him up.

But Macpherson cheated it.

"Don't look down," he told himself, and inch by inch he edged himself along the ledge, trying not to think of what might happen if his foot slipped.

At last! He had reached the right spot. Now all he had to do was stretch up and give the trembling sheep a push from behind. *Heave-ho!* But it was not as easy as all that. Macpherson had no idea a sheep could be so heavy, or so stubborn. There she was in peril of her life, and what did she do to help herself? Not a thing. Indeed, she seemed to be resisting his efforts to push her.

"Come on, silly!" shouted Macpherson. "Move!"

He pushed, he shoved, he heaved. And at last she began to move. He had done it. She was back on safe ground. Another success for Macpherson the Brave.

A bark from the dog as if to say, "Well done, Macpherson." And now the sheep was wandering away, cropping the grass between the tufts of heather as if nothing had happened. Just like wee Maisie Murphy, crying her eyes out one minute and sucking happily at a lollipop the next.

Macpherson grinned, feeling on top of the

world. All he had to do now was give himself one big heave and he, too, would be over the top and back on firm ground.

"Heave-ho, Macpherson!"

He was almost up and over the top when the rocky ledge crumbled and gave way under his feet. Macpherson gave a cry of alarm and clung with all his might to a clump of sea-pinks growing from the side of a rock.

"Help! Hold me!"

He had no idea what he was saying. And how could the sea-pinks help him? They broke off under his grasp, and now there was nothing to support him. Down he fell. Down, down, scurrying against the side of the cliff, stretching out his hands in vain for something to clutch. But there was nothing. Only the wild waves waiting for him below.

Then suddenly one of Macpherson's miracles happened. His feet came to rest on another ledge, far down near the surface of the sea. He was safe, at least for the moment.

The startled sea-birds screamed at him, circling over his head as if they wanted to shoo him out of their way. Different birds from the city sparrows or the ducks Macpherson had seen in the park at home. These were puffins, oyster-catchers, guillemots and seagulls. All noisily complaining at this creature from Outer Space who had dropped from the sky to disturb their peace.

Why had he come? To catch and kill them? Or was he one of those strange humans who came stalking them with cameras, prying into their habits, finding out where they had nested and how many eggs they laid?

For a time they kept on circling and squawking. Then, finding the boy harmless, they settled back on their perches on the rocks and left him alone. Whoever he was, it was obvious he had no intention of hurting them.

Macpherson was too dazed even to notice them. His knees were bruised and bleeding, his jersey was torn, but what did that matter? He was safe. At least until the sea came nearer and swallowed him up.

Suddenly he realised that the tide was coming in. Every wave was swirling farther up the rocks. Soon the ledge on which he was standing would be swamped, and then what would happen to him? It was all very well for the puffins and oyster-catchers. They had only to flap their wings and fly away. But what about him? It was impossible to try climbing back up the cliff. He was trapped.

An anxious bark from up above. Macpher-

son, careful not to overbalance, peered
cautiously up the cliff-side. Mercy me! What a
height! Had he tumbled down all *that* way?
Rusty was there at the top barking at him as if
sending down a message. And now the barks
sounded farther off as if the dog was running
away and leaving him to his fate. Or maybe —

yes! That's what he would be doing, a sensible dog like Rusty. Running off to Big Hamish to get help.

Macpherson began to feel better. Big Hamish would know what to do. If only he got here in time. The tide was coming in faster now, the big waves splashing the spray up into his face. He could taste the salt water on his lips. Hurry, Rusty, hurry!

A sound from the distance. The skirl of the bagpipes, wasn't it? Yes! Of course. That's what Big Hamish was up to; having a practice on the pipes. Macpherson remembered now. Big Hamish McTavish was to play tonight at the dinner-party at the Castle, marching round and round the table to entertain Sir George and his guests. And he — Macpherson — was to be one of the guests. That is, if the sea didn't swallow him up first.

He had been specially invited. *Your presence is requested at dinner tonight at Glen Bogle Castle.* Fancy dining in a Castle! And who knew? Maybe he would see the ghost.

"Man, Macpherson, *there*'s an honour," Big Hamish had said in his great booming voice, thumping the boy on the back. "You'll need to put on your best kilt."

"I've only got the one," Macpherson confessed. And a shabby one it was, too. Far too short and skimpy for him, and all the colours faded.

"Wait now, Macpherson."

A change had come over the big man's face. A sad look was in his eyes, and there was a different note in his voice when he spoke. "I'm thinking you might as well have Angus's. It's never been on. I bought it for the lad but he never wore it."

Macpherson had wondered about the lad and why Big Hamish lived all alone in the whitewashed cottage. He had not liked to ask about the photograph on the mantelpiece. Who was the woman with the gentle face and who was the boy who looked the very image of Hamish McTavish? He had a twinkle in his eyes, as if he had a funny-bone like Macpherson's. It would have been fun to have the likes of him for a playmate. But where was he and why did Big Hamish never talk about him?

But now that the ice was broken, Big Hamish talked about him as he rummaged in the cupboard looking for the kilt.

"He was about your age — Angus — when he died. And I lost the wife, too, both in the same week. It was the epidemic . . ."

Macpherson listened in silence with a great

lump in his throat, not knowing what to say. He was not too sure what an epidemic was. The 'flu, maybe. Or something worse. Whatever it was, it had brought tragedy to the whitewashed cottage and left Big Hamish with only a photograph and his sad memories.

He had found the kilt by now and was opening out the parcel, with a strange look on his face. "He was going to wear it on the Sunday," he said sadly. "But by then . . ."

Macpherson tried to swallow the lump in his throat. "It's a fine kilt," he gulped and stretched out, not for the kilt but for Hamish's rough hand. It was a gesture of sympathy, a way of showing all he wanted to say but couldn't find words for. Big Hamish knew and understood. He gripped Macpherson's hand firmly.

"Ay, it's a fine kilt." He turned hastily away not to let Macpherson see the look in his eyes. Ay! And more than a look. Big Hamish of Glen Bogle was in tears. Then he shook himself as if he were Rusty and suddenly he was back to normal.

"Come on, Macpherson," he boomed. "Try it on and see how it fits."

It fitted all right. It might have been made for him instead of the lad on the mantelpiece.

And somehow, once he was inside it, the sad moment was gone and Macpherson had enough sense not to speak of it again.

"Oh jings!" he said, twirling round and round so that the kilt could swirl with him. "I'm awful pleased with it, Mr Hamish, sir. It's great! I'll be as careful with it as can be."

"Ay, well, you'd better take it off now, Macpherson, and get back into your old togs till it's time for the dinner. I'm away to practise the pipes."

So that was why the faint faraway strains of *Highland Laddie* were now reaching Macpherson's ears as he clung for his life to the cliff-side with the sea swirling over his feet. As long as he heard the sound there was no hope of being rescued, for it was only Big Hamish who could save him. And suddenly Macpherson felt sorry for the big man rather than for himself. Wouldn't it be a terrible thing for Hamish to lose *two* lads and the kilt never once being worn? Would there be one empty seat at Sir George's dinner-table at Glen Bogle Castle tonight?

Look out, Macpherson! Danger!

Macpherson forgot about the kilt and the bagpipes and everything else. A new terror was threatening him, even more frightening than the waves. Why had the sea-birds suddenly taken wing and gone screaming out over the water? Something was swooping down on them from the sky. Something large and fierce that was flapping its great wings and uttering strange cries.

Good gracious! It was the great muckle bird Macpherson had seen hovering high up near its eyrie on the mountain top. But now it had come down, swooping and whirling, as if about to attack him.

With a cold feeling of horror at his heart, he remembered what Big Hamish had told him about the giant bird that lived high up in the mountain, how it swooped down on helpless animals, pecked out their eyes, clutched them in its great claws and carried them off to devour in its nest.

The eagle had taken some of Hamish's lambs. Had it now come to take Macpherson?

He was helpless. How could he hope to fight off such a powerful enemy? The sea was swirling over his knees by now. It would soon be up to his waist, and then to his neck, and then over his head. Or would the big bird carry him off first?

The eagle seemed to be dive-bombing him, missing him only by inches. He could feel the *swish-sh-sh* of its wings as it took sudden darts and swoops past him. Then it circled and turned as if getting the measure of its target. Nearer and nearer . . .

"Grandpa! Help!"

Macpherson let out a sudden frenzied call of despair. Not to his slaves, but to Grandpa far away in Glasgow. "Grandpa! Grandpa! HELP!"

He did not know that help was coming, that the music had stopped and that Big Hamish, with Rusty barking and bounding ahead of him, was running up the hillside with a rope in his hand. He only knew that the sea was coming higher and the big bird nearer. And all he wanted at the end of his life was to feel Grandpa's wrinkled hand in his.

"*Grandpa!*"

And then, as if in a dream, he heard a voice shouting to him. Was it Grandpa's or Big Hamish's?

"Hold on, Macpherson! I'll have you up in a jiffy."

5

Ghosts and Witches

"Man, Macpherson, you look splendid. It suits you a treat. Ay! a real treat."

Big Hamish spoke in a huskier voice than usual as he looked at Macpherson and tried to avoid the gaze of the lad on the mantelpiece.

Macpherson was wearing the kilt. With his terrifying adventure behind him and his bruised knees patched up, he was getting ready to go with his host to Glen Bogle Castle.

It was a fine feeling to be on firm ground again with the danger over. To forget how near he had been to death, and to be wearing a brand-new kilt that made him look somebody. It was a pity Grandpa couldn't see him now, and wee Maisie Murphy. He could almost hear her saying, "Oh Macpherthon, you look ever tho great". True enough, he felt great.

Until he saw the look in Big Hamish's eyes. Then his own face clouded. Inwardly he began to scold himself. Selfish thing! What right had *he* to feel great? Had he not been frightened

out of his wits only a wee while ago? There
had been nothing great about him then. A
fearty, that's what he had been, bawling for
Grandpa with tears rolling down his cheeks as
if he was a lassie.

And now here he was strutting about in his
new kilt as if he was King of the Castle. And
all the time it should have been the lad in the
picture who was wearing it. *He* would have
looked a treat in it all right.

"It's a shame," he blurted out, trying to
convey his feelings to the big man. "Oh Mr
Hamish, sir, if only . . . if only *he* . . ."

"Hoots!" Big Hamish turned round and
gave him a great thump on the back to show
that he understood. "I'm thinking the lad's
pleased. Come on, Macpherson. We'll need to
step out or Sir George'll be on the rampage."
And once more the sadness was over and
everything back to normal.

As they walked up the drive towards the
Castle, Macpherson tried to lengthen his stride
to keep up with Hamish. But it was impossible. The big man's steps were like Jack the
Giant-Killer's. The only way to keep pace with
him was to run.

"Mercy me!" Macpherson suddenly
stopped in his tracks and let out a cry of

surprise. "Oh look, Mr Hamish, sir! It's like a castle in a fairy-tale."

So it seemed with its towers and turrets twisting up to the sky. Its old moat and drawbridge. And the ramparts where the ghost was said to walk in the moonlight. What tales it could tell of strange happenings in the past! Mary, Queen of Scots — the sad queen — had once looked wistfully out of the tower window, with her four Maries in attendance. Bonnie Prince Charlie himself had sought refuge here when he was fleeing from his enemies.

It was all in the history books. And now Macpherson was joining the ranks of the great. *He* was crossing the drawbridge, following the footsteps of kings and queens into Glen Bogle Castle.

"Wake up, boy, and tell us all about it."

Sir George Stuart, cigar in hand, leaned back in his chair and looked at Macpherson with a friendly twinkling glance.

Macpherson sat up with a jerk. True enough, he had almost been asleep, sitting at the great round table where royalty had once fed. No wonder he had felt drowsy after all the good food he had eaten. Never before had he seen so many knives, forks and spoons. Never before had he tasted such strange delicious dishes. And the company! There were real lords and ladies — Sir George's grand friends — sitting round the table. And there was Annabelle in a white gown with sparkling jewels at her neck, looking more than ever like a princess.

What a time to feel sleepy! It was not only the effect of the food but of the strong sea air and his afternoon adventure which had nearly cost him his life. And the haunting strains of the bagpipes as Big Hamish marched round the table, playing an old sad tune. If Macpherson let himself go, he would lay his head down on the polished table and drift off into dreamland.

Sir George's voice brought him back to his senses. And Annabelle's. "Oh yes, Macpherson. Do tell us."

She spoke eagerly and her eyes were shining as she leaned across the table, all white and glittering. "You always have *such* adventures. And you're so brave."

Brave! He squared his shoulders, seeing himself through her eyes. Macpherson the Brave who could fight off eagles and push back the angry sea without turning a hair. Och! He was brave all right. Braver than . . .

Suddenly he seemed to hear Grandpa's warning voice. "Stick to the truth, Macpherson. The truth!"

A flush came over Macpherson's face. Then he did the bravest thing of all. He told the truth.

"It was *him*," he said, pointing to Big Hamish marching round the table. "He's a hero. I'm just a . . . a f-f-fearty!"

It was a terrible confession to make in front of Annabelle and Sir George and all the fine lords and ladies. Macpherson hung his head in shame and waited for the blow to fall. Instead, Sir George threw back his head and gave a great guffaw, dropping cigar-ash on the table.

"Ha-ha-ha! Don't you worry, Macpherson," he cried, his eyes brimming with laughter. "It happens to the best of us. A fearty, eh? Goodness! Many's the time I've felt the same. A fearty! Ha-ha-ha!"

The lords and ladies laughed with him. Hamish broke into a livelier tune and quickened his step, while Macpherson gazed at the great man — his host — with surprise and relief. Fancy Sir George being afraid of anything or anybody! It just showed you. You never knew what went on inside anybody, no matter how great they were.

"Come along, Macpherson. Let's go and explore the Castle." Annabelle held out a white inviting hand to him.

"Yes, off you go, you two." Sir George nodded approvingly. "And don't disturb the ghost. A fearty, eh!"

"I bet you weren't *really* afraid," said Annabelle as they went through the great hall, hung with trophies, and up the stairway to the gallery. "Were you, Macpherson?"

"Well . . . a wee bit," admitted Macpherson and hastily changed the subject. "Where's the ghost?"

"Look! There she is."

"Where?" cried Macpherson, startled.

Annabelle laughed. She was pointing to a portrait hanging on the wall beside others of her long-dead ancestors. A painting of a slender figure in a long white gown, with hair like Annabelle's and the same large wistful eyes.

"Mercy! Is *she* the ghost? She looks just like you, Annabelle."

"Yes, I'm named after her and everybody says we look alike. But I don't walk in the moonlight."

"Do you — do you think we'll see her tonight?" asked Macpherson, half-hoping, half-fearing.

"No, no, it's too dark. She only comes when the moon shines."

"Why does she do it?" wondered Macpherson, gazing up at the white lady.

"She's said to be looking for Bonnie Prince Charlie. She helped him to escape, you know. Never mind, Macpherson. Let's leave this gloomy old gallery. It always gives me the shivers. There's heaps more to see."

Macpherson, swinging his kilt, followed her. He, too, was glad to get away from the gallery. There *was* something shivery about it. He had been a fearty once today and that was enough for him. All the same, it was difficult to feel brave with ghosts about. Annabelle looked like one herself, gliding along the corridors in front of him in her white dress, swooping round corners and disappearing up and down stairs. What a great muckle place the Castle was! He would have been lost without her to guide him.

"I'm so glad you've come, Macpherson," she said, turning to beckon him on. "Uncle's guests are all so old and dull. You're different."

"Ay, I'm different." Macpherson strutted a

little. All his self-confidence had come back.

"I say, Macpherson . . ." They were on their way back towards the gallery when Annabelle suddenly had an idea. "Let's go and visit the witch tomorrow."

"What?" Macpherson stopped in his tracks. Ghosts were bad enough, but witches . . .

"Yes, a real witch. She lives in a cottage away up the glen. I've always wanted to go and visit her but I've never dared. You'll take me tomorrow, won't you, Macpherson?"

"Well . . ." Jings! Fancy getting mixed up with witches. It would take a million years to tell Grandpa all his adventures when he got back to Glasgow. "Okay!" he said boldly. "We'll go and see her tomorrow."

"Goody!" Annabelle gave a little jump of excitement. "We'll take a picnic and . . ."

Macpherson wasn't listening. He was standing stockstill in terror, gaping in front of him. What was that coming towards them, gliding along in the shadows of the gallery? Something white, something unearthly, something silent was coming nearer, nearer . . . It was the ghost!

Annabelle had seen it, too. She caught her breath and clutched at Macpherson for protection. Protection! His knees were shaking, he was trembling all over, and his heart was thud-thudding like the beating of a drum. But Annabelle was clinging trustingly to him. Macpherson the Brave. *He* must protect her.

He braced himself and summoned up all his courage. Never mind his slaves. This was something he had to do himself. As the ghost came nearer, he could hear her breathing. He had not known that ghosts breathed, but there was a lot he was learning at Glen Bogle.

Brace yourself, Macpherson! What did one say to ghosts? Macpherson stood his ground and cried in the bravest voice he could muster, "S-Stand and deliver!"

The words echoed round the gallery and came back to him in his own muffled voice. "S-Stand and deliver!"

And then the ghost spoke.

"So there you are, Miss Annabelle. I've been looking for you all over the place. And that boy! I might have known *he* would be leading you into trouble."

It was Mrs Alexander, the housekeeper — White Apron, Macpherson called her. He had met her before in Sir George's big house in Glasgow, and she was not a bit pleased to see him here. She and Old Skinflint had one thing in common. They both agreed that boys were pests! Now she came bearing down on him like an angry hen looking for her chick.

White Apron! Macpherson began to laugh through sheer relief, and the whole gallery laughed with him, echoing his merriment. All except White Apron. She was not amused.

"You come along at once, Miss Annabelle," she said firmly. "It's high time you were in bed. And as for you!" She glared at Macpherson. "You'd better take yourself off. That big man, Hamish, is waiting for you downstairs. I've had enough of him, too, with his noisy bagpipes. A fine pair you are!"

Macpherson obediently took himself off, but not before Annabelle had whispered to him, "Tomorrow! Don't forget."

Macpherson didn't forget. That was why he and Annabelle were now scrambling up the glen, carrying a large picnic-basket between them with Rusty bounding in front, blazing the trail.

Macpherson would have liked to follow him more quickly. Two things held him back. The weight of the basket and the fact that Annabelle had to stop every few yards to get back her breath. She was delicate. Not like Maisie Murphy who would have said, "Thee how fatht I can go! Hurry up, Macpherthon. Let'th run to the top."

Annabelle was more accustomed to being driven in Sir George's great car by Smithers, the chauffeur, than walking so far over such rough ground. Macpherson looked anxiously at her and slowed his pace to suit hers.

"Let me have the basket. I'll carry it by myself."

"No, no; it's too heavy." Annabelle struggled on for a few more yards, then gave it up. "Let's stop for a rest. It's time we had our picnic, anyway. I wonder what Mrs Alexander has put in the basket?"

They soon found out. Though White Apron was not fond of boys, she knew all about their open-air appetites. And though Macpherson had eaten more than his fill last night he was now as hungry as a hunter.

No doubt about it he was feeling the benefit of his Highland holiday. His freckled face was tanned and healthy-looking, and already he seemed to have grown bigger and broader.

Big Hamish had remarked on it at breakfast that morning after Macpherson had finished his second helping of porridge.

"I'm thinking you'll turn out to be a giant yet, Macpherson. Och ay! You'll be tossing the caber at the Highland Games."

That was another treat Macpherson had in store. They were getting ready at Glen Bogle for the one great event of the year: the

Highland Games. People came from far and near, on bicycles and in buses, cars and coaches to see the big fellows tossing the caber, throwing the hammer and putting the shot; to hear the pipers competing against each other and to watch the dancers doing the Highland Fling.

There were to be pole vaults, high jumps, long jumps and goodness knows what. There was even to be one event in which Macpherson himself was taking part: the Hundred Yards for Youths.

He was a youth all right, but some of the other competitors were years older as well as bigger and brawnier. All the same, he had been practising every day on the flat stretch of grass behind the whitewashed cottage while Big Hamish tried his hand at tossing the caber. Macpherson was amazed at the big man's strength. *He* could not even lift the great telegraph-pole into an upright position, far less toss it.

"Stick to your porridge, Macpherson," the great man told him, "and you'll beat us all yet."

Meantime Macpherson stuck to the hundred yards with Rusty racing against him for competition. He was getting faster every day. Wouldn't it be a fine thing if he won and had his name in the paper, and a prize to carry home to Grandpa?

Ho-ro! Up she rises!

No wonder Macpherson felt happy as he sat down on the heather beside the picnic-basket. What a peaceful place this was compared to the big busy city. Miles of sky to be seen and never a sound except the swish of the sea in the distance and the call of the curlew overhead. Away high up on the mountain he could see the big bird. The eagle that had caused him such terror yesterday.

Today was different. The bird was far away and he was safe sitting beside Annabelle, waiting hungrily for her to open the basket.

"Look, Macpherson! Chicken and ham and pies and fruit and chocolate biscuits and lemonade. Enough for a regiment."

"Jings!" Macpherson licked his lips. "Let's set to."

They set to, Macpherson eating the major share. Never mind the regiment. He could manage fine himself.

When he came to the chocolate biscuits he thought of Grandpa and his sweet tooth, wishing he could put one of the biscuits in his pocket to save for the old man. Though he was enjoying his holiday, he missed Grandpa at every turn of the day. And wee Maisie Murphy, too.

"I'll have to send Grandpa another postcard," he thought, carefully taking off the silver paper to save for a Guide Dog back in Glasgow. "He'll have got that one already, the one with the Highland cows on it."

He could imagine Grandpa taking it to the window to see it better, peering at it through the magnifying-glass he used when he was working on his ships-in-bottles.

"See this, Janet woman," he would call to Aunt Janet, clattering about in the kitchen. "It's a card from Macpherson. From Glen Bogle."

"Tuts!" Aunt Janet would pretend not to care, but she would be interested all right. "What does the boy say?" And then Grandpa would tell her, slowly reading out the words Macpherson had written in his very best hand.

"Hope you and Aunt Janet are in the pink. I'm fine, but I'm missing you, Grandpa. Wish you were here. Tell Maisie I was asking for her. Macpherson."

Wish you were here! There was always something left to wish for. That was the way of the world. Though, mind you, he was lucky, and none knew it better than himself as he sat back and sighed. "I'm full up!"

"Look, Macpherson, away up there."

"Where?"

Annabelle was pointing far up the glen. "There! That's the witch's cottage. Oh, Macpherson, I wonder if we dare?"

"Dare? Hoots ay!"

In broad daylight and after such a feed Macpherson would have dared anything. What was a witch to him? Had he not got the better of dragons and monsters in his day? That was the worst of lasses. They were as bold as brass when it came to suggesting things. Not so bold when it came to carrying them out.

Macpherson began to tidy up the picnic-basket in a businesslike manner. "Let's leave it here," he suggested sensibly, "and get it on the way back." There was still plenty of food left, enough for another good meal. "Maybe we could have a bite on the way down."

"All right, Macpherson," agreed Annabelle meekly. He was the boss, arranging everything for her, helping her up the hill, showing her the safest places to step. Now and then he darted off to try his hundred yards' sprint wherever there was an even piece of ground.

But soon the climb grew steeper, and even Rusty had to stop for breath, puffing and panting with his tongue hanging out.

It was a slow process. Macpherson had to help Annabelle up, step by step. Then suddenly she gave a cry — louder than the curlew's — and sank to the ground like a butterfly with a broken wing.

"Oh Macpherson!" she wailed. "My ankle."

Macpherson crouched down beside her, full of concern. "What's happened? Is it broken?"

"Just twisted, I think. Help me up."

Macpherson tried to prop her up, but she sank back once more on her heathery cushion, wincing with pain. Then, seeing the anxious look on Macpherson's face, she gave a little smile and said bravely, "Don't worry, Macpherson. I'll try hopping on one foot."

"No, you won't! How can you hop up this steep hill? It's bad enough walking. What you need is a . . ." What was it? He searched his mind trying to remember what Aunt Janet had put on his ankle the day he tumbled off a lorry. "Oh yes! A cold compress. And a bandage."

Annabelle looked amused, in spite of her pain. "And where d'you think you'll get them?

In the heather?''

"There!"

He pointed to the brow of the hill. Until he looked up he had not realised how near they were to the witch's cottage. It was only a short steep climb away.

"But what about her? The witch!" Annabelle gave a shiver.

"Och! Never heed her." Macpherson had more important things to think about than witches. He gave his orders, first to the dog. "You stay there, Rusty, and keep guard." Then to Annabelle, "Don't move. I'll be back in a twinkling."

He put his words into action, sprinting away up the hill as if trying to beat his own record. Never noticing how steep it was. But though his feet were light, his heart was heavy with guilt. What had he done? He ought never to have allowed Annabelle to come on this foolhardy climb. Supposing she never walked again! What would Sir George and White Apron say? It was all his fault.

Before he knew where he was, he was pushing open the witch's gate, if it could be called a gate. Part of an old iron bedstead. It creaked eerily as he swung it open and ran up the overgrown garden path. He had no time to take in more than a quick impression. Of neglected flowers struggling for growth through a tangle of nettles and weeds. Of cocks and hens cackling on the doorstep. Of cracked window-panes and broken slates. Of a lean cat spitting at him from the window-sill. Worst of all, of a croaking voice calling, "Who's there?"

It was the witch! For a moment Macpherson's footsteps faltered. His impulse was to turn and run for his life, away from this uncanny house and the terrifying creature inside. He could be out of the garden gate in a jiffy and back down the hillside before the witch was any wiser.

Then he remembered the look of pain on Annabelle's pale face and forgot his own fears. He had come for help, and he was going to get it no matter what it cost.

Squaring himself up, he stepped past the cocks and hens, pushed the door wide open and marched in to meet the witch.

6

Danger from the Sky

The first thing Macpherson saw was her broomstick propped up in a dark dusty corner.

Then his eyes rested on the witch herself. She was sitting bolt upright in an old rocking-chair staring at him with black piercing eyes. Her face was lined and wrinkled with age. Her grey hair straggled untidily over her forehead, and she was dressed in black musty garments which any scarecrow might have scorned. Her fingers were knotted and twisted, and she tightened them on the sides of the chair as Macpherson approached.

Suddenly, to his surprise, the chair began to move. She was rocking herself forward to meet him.

The cat, spitting with rage, took a flying leap from the window-sill and landed in her lap. The cocks and hens came cackling and clucking to her feet as if ranging themselves against the intruder.

Macpherson stood his ground, though his

knees were knocking.

"Who's there?" said the witch in her croaking voice. "What do you want?"

The creaking chair came rocking towards him but Macpherson still stood firm. He could see a tap and a basin in the little kitchen beyond. That was what he wanted. Cold water for a compress and some bandages to take the pain from Annabelle's ankle.

"Excuse me," he began. And then blurted out his story. The witch stopped her rocking to listen to him. All about Annabelle and how she must have help, and how this was the only cottage within reach.

"Could I have some cold water and some bandages?" he ended. "Please!"

The cat spat at him, baring its teeth like a wild beast. One of the cocks pecked viciously at his ankles, and the witch fixed him with a piercing gaze. Was she going to cast an evil spell on him? Or mount her broomstick and ride away?

He braced himself for the worst. Then, to his surprise, a change came over her wrinkled face. She began to smile! It was a toothless smile, but it made all the difference in the gloomy little room. As if someone had switched on a cheerful light.

The cat started to purr instead of spit. The cocks and hens cackled in a friendly fashion, and Macpherson, heaving a sigh of relief, made a sudden discovery. This was no witch. She was only a lonely neglected woman, racked with rheumatism and unable to move except with the aid of her rocking-chair.

"Mercy me!" he cried, staring at her with sudden recognition. "You're Old Morag!"

"Yes, that's me. Old Morag." She peered closer at him. "And how would you be knowing?"

It was all coming back to Macpherson. The tales he had heard while he sat drowsing at the peat-fire in the whitewashed cottage, with Big Hamish smoking his pipe and talking to him at the end of the day. Sometimes Macpherson nodded off, tired with the day's adventures in the open air, and lost the thread. The stories became all mixed up in his mind when he half-remembered them next day.

He was trying to untangle one of them now, a tale about an old woman who lived far up the glen and who had the second sight.

"What's that?" he had asked Big Hamish, trying not to yawn.

"The second sight? Och! It's a kind of power."

"Like Rusty has with the sheep?"

"Ay, something the same. Only Old Morag can see into the future."

"Fancy!"

Macpherson had tried to force his eyes wide open, but he drifted away again and only half-heard the rest of the story. Snatches of it stuck in his mind.

"Keeps herself to herself. Doesn't like visitors. But the lad used to go and see her. Angus." Big Hamish looked at the photograph on the mantelpiece. "She liked *him*. What's more, she warned me. Said he would never grow up to be a man. I'll maybe take a turn up the the glen to see her. Old Morag. Second sight . . ."

Macpherson was recalling it all as he faced the old woman in the rocking-chair.

"It was Big Hamish," he told her. "I'm staying with him."

"But you're not Angus."

She peered forward, her face suddenly lighting up.

"No, I'm Macpherson from Glasgow. I'm here on my holidays."

Strange to be talking away like this to a witch and her not casting a spell on him. Could she see into his future? What did her second sight tell her? Was *he* to grow up to be a man? Become a famous doctor, maybe? Or an explorer? Or even the Lord Provost of Glasgow?

"Glasgow," said Old Morag in a faraway voice, as if Glasgow was in another world. "And you want bandages for the lassie?"

The lassie! Goodness! A fine doctor *he*'d make. He had forgotten all about his patient and her need for urgent attention.

"Oh yes, please," he said guiltily. "I'd be very grateful if I could have some, and may I take a basin of cold water with me?"

"Away and help yourself."

Old Morag went rocking round the kitchen till she came to a cupboard in the corner. Opening the door she took out an old pillow-case and tore it into strips, while Macpherson hurried into the untidy back-kitchen to fill the basin with water. As he did so, he looked about him wondering how the old woman managed to survive in such an isolated place. There was little food to be seen. Only the end of a stale loaf of bread and some cheese that was covered with green mould. No wonder she looked so thin and ill. She must be half-starving.

There was a great feeling of pity in his heart

as he came back to her and asked, "How do you get on? I mean, about shopping and food?"

"Shopping?" The idea seemed to amuse her so much that she gave a kind of crooked smile. "Where would I be finding shops here? The grocer's van comes to the foot of the hill, but I can't get down nowadays. Sometimes the van-man sends some groceries up, or the postman brings them. But they often forget. The lad used to come. Angus . . ."

Her eyes filled with tears as she spoke of him. And Macpherson, swallowing a lump in his throat, made a resolution. He would try to take the lad's place. He would see that the old woman was not left lonely and neglected any longer. He would gather sticks and peat for her fire. He would get Big Hamish to come up and mend the leaks in the roof and the cracks in the window-panes. And there was something he could do for her right now as soon as he had attended to Annabelle. He would bring up the picnic-basket and leave its contents for Old Morag to eat.

"I'll be back," he promised, taking the bandages from her twisted fingers. "Many thanks. You're a friend in need. Cheerio!"

"Cheerio!"

She watched him go, rocking herself to the door to see him out of sight. A friend in need! "Yes," she said, stroking the cat on her lap. "*He*'ll be back!"

"Oh, Macpherson, I thought you were never coming," cried Annabelle when he reached her side. "What was the witch like? Terrible? Did she try to put you in her pot, or cast a spell over you? Oh, Macpherson you *are* brave."

"Hoots!" said Macpherson, not liking to deny it. All the same, he told Annabelle the truth while she looked up at him with large wondering eyes.

"The poor old thing!" she cried, when he came to the bit about the picnic-basket. "Yes, of course, you must take it to her. At once."

He shook his head. "Not till I've patched you up. How's the ankle?"

"Not bad." But he could tell by the drawn look on her pale face that she was suffering. "The poor old thing!" she repeated, not thinking of herself but of the lonely old woman in the rocking-chair. "And us imagining her a witch! I must go and visit her as soon as I can, and I'll ask Uncle to send Smithers up with some milk and butter and fruit . . ."

"Steady!" said Macpherson, busy with the cold compresses. He was dipping the bandages in water, squeezing them out and applying them to Annabelle's swollen ankle with all the gentleness and skill of a trained doctor. "How does that feel?"

"Much better." Annabelle smiled to reassure him. "You *are* clever, Macpherson."

"Hoots!" he said, pretending to deny it, but he was pleased, all the same. "There!" he said, having completed his doctoring, "that'll do till you get back home."

"But how am I to get down the hill?" asked Annabelle, looking first at her bandaged ankle and then at the steep path they had climbed.

"I'll carry you," said Macpherson.

And why not? She was no heavier than the message-baskets he often had to carry to Old Skinflint's customers. But Annabelle would not hear of it.

"Nonsense! Not all that distance. You'd better go down by yourself, Macpherson, and send up Smithers and Hamish. They can carry me turn about. And tell Uncle not to worry."

"Okay," agreed Macpherson, taking his commands; but it was he who was worried. Would it be safe to leave Annabelle up here all by herself and her looking so pale and helpless?

"Rusty'll stay with me," she said, guessing his thoughts. "And, Macpherson, you'd better take the food up to the old woman first."

"Righto!" Macpherson picked up the picnic-basket and the empty basin, then darted off like an arrow from a bow, as if heavy weights meant nothing to him. Big Hamish was right. Just wait! He would be tossing the caber before long.

Old Morag had been watching and waiting for him. She was at the door, rocking to and fro, with the cocks and hens at her feet and the cat in her lap.

"I knew you'd come back," she greeted him. "How's the lassie?"

"Fine!" panted Macpherson, glad to lay down his burden, thankful that his caber-tossing exploits were in the future. "I'm away down to get help from the men."

"Ay!" The old woman nodded her head and looked far away into the distance. "Better not waste time," she said in a strange voice. "There's danger coming from the sky."

Danger! Macpherson looked at her in alarm, remembering about the second sight and how she could see into the future. What danger could come from the sky? What was she staring at? Was it the big eagle away up in its eyrie? That black cloud, maybe, or something beyond it? Something sinister that ordinary eyes could not see?

"I'll hurry," he promised. "See, I've brought some food for you." He opened the basket, trying to keep the cocks and hens and the hungry cat from snatching at its contents.

"Food!" said Old Morag in a quavery voice. Her dim eyes lit up as she looked at the chicken, the ham, the pies, the biscuits. "It's a feast!"

"I'll put the basket on the table where you can reach it, with the lid ready to open," said Macpherson, being practical. "And I'll come back as soon as I can and get a fire going and do some odd jobs."

"Just like *him* — Angus! Always so kind. Never forgetting Old Morag."

The shaky old hand came out and Macpherson grasped it warmly in his. "I won't forget," he promised stoutly. Wasn't it strange how he was always getting mixed up with that other boy? He had a funny feeling he was only half-Macpherson, half-Angus.

But he was himself all right when he sped down the hillside with Old Morag's final warning ringing in his ears. "Danger coming from the sky!" He did not wait to waste words with Annabelle and Rusty when he reached them. "Cheerio!" he called out and went flying past, his mind busy with all the things he must do.

He would go to the Big House first. To Glen Bogle Castle, and break the news to Sir George. Then he would have to tell White Apron, and a fine fuss *she* would make. After that he would run to the whitewashed cottage to seek help from Big Hamish and to get milk and butter for Old Morag. No time to waste. Danger was coming from the sky!

It came when the rescue-party was only half-way up the glen. Until now Macpherson had been enjoying the expedition. He was the important one, walking in front and leading the way. Macpherson the World-famous Explorer.

" 'Ere! 'Old on, Macpherson, me old cock sparrer," panted Smithers, more at home behind the wheel of Sir George's great car than on a rough hillside. "Blimey! This ain't 'alf a steep climb, this ain't 'alf. Me feet's killing me."

Big Hamish let out a great booming laugh. "I'm thinking you'll not do so well at the Highland Games, Mr Smithers. Not unless you put in a bit of training."

" 'Ighland Games!" scoffed Smithers, slithering backwards. "A lot of 'eathens, with them hawful bagpipes and them 'orrible 'aggises."

" 'Aggises?" queried Big Hamish, lending him a helping hand.

"He means *haggises*," translated Macpherson.

"Haggises. The very thing you're needing, Mr Smithers," grinned Hamish. "Put some muscle on you."

"Me muscles is hokay," grumbled Smithers. "It's me feet."

Big Hamish gave another laugh, but this time it was drowned by a louder sound. A thunderclap that crashed overhead with such a sudden explosion that it seemed to split the sky in two.

"Jings!" gasped Macpherson, turning pale. "Danger from the sky!"

" 'Elp!" cried Smithers, staring up at the sky. "If this ain't the last straw!"

"Toots! It's only a thunderstorm," said Hamish calmly. "It'll clear the air. Been working up to it all day."

"Better 'urry and get Miss Hannabelle," said Smithers, forgetting his own troubles and

pressing forward with greater determination. "Don't like thunder, she doesn't." There came another crash from overhead. "Can't say as 'ow I care much for it meself."

"Speed on, Macpherson," boomed Big Hamish. "I'm thinking we can't be far off now."

"No, not far," said Macpherson, scrambling over a boulder. "This way."

He was no longer thinking of his own honour and glory. Only of reaching Annabelle before the storm broke. Already it was gathering force. Sudden flashes of lightning came sizzling from the sky followed by loud crashes of thunder, as if all the clouds were cracking their heads together. It was like being in a battle. As if the whole of Glen Bogle was under bombardment from the air.

Then: "Oh mercy me! Here comes the rain!" cried Macpherson in consternation.

No ordinary rain. It fell first in big blobs so thick that they were almost solid.

"Coo! Right down me neck," cried Smithers, turning up his collar.

Then came the real rain. Such rain as Macpherson had never seen before even on the wettest day in Glasgow. It was almost as if a waterfall was tumbling down on top of them. And all the time the thunderstorm gathered force overhead. *Flash-crack! Flash-crack!*

Macpherson's breath was taken away. Blinded by the rain, deafened by the thunder, he could not hear what Hamish was shouting at him. He could only see that the big man was urging him onward, hauling Smithers to his feet when he stumbled, and trying to keep his own feet as firmly as he could on the wet ground.

The rain was running in rivulets down the glen. Annabelle must be drenched to the skin, sitting helpless on the wet heather with no hope of shelter. "Annabelle!" cried Macpherson, stumbling and slithering as he forced his way forward, peering through the rain to get his first glimpse of her.

At last! Thank goodness, he had reached the spot.

"It's all right, Annabelle. We're here!"

There was no reply. Macpherson stopped and caught his breath in alarm.

She was not there!

7

Lost and Found

"Not 'ere!" cried Smithers in alarm.

"Not here!" echoed Big Hamish, wiping the rain from his face. "But where can she be? I thought her ankle was hurt."

"So it is," said Macpherson in a daze. "She can't have gone far. How could she walk?"

At the back of his mind he was recalling another search-party, in the park, for wee Maisie Murphy. He had found her all right. Oh, please, let him find Annabelle.

"Will she 'ave gone and tumbled into one of them there ravines?" suggested Smithers, almost tumbling into one himself. "Blimey! I ain't never seen such an 'eathenish place. Poor Miss Hannabelle. And 'er so delicate. This'll be the death of 'er even if she's alive."

"Of course she's alive," shouted Big Hamish between cracks of thunder. He had seen the stricken look on Macpherson's face, and gave the boy a reassuring smile.

"Rusty was with her. He'd keep her safe,"

95

said Macpherson, trying to convince himself.

"*Rusty!*"

Hamish let out a great roar and followed it with a piercing whistle, trying to make himself heard above the fury of the storm. *Shout-whistle! Flash-crack! Shout-whistle!*

Suddenly Macpherson held up his hand as if to still the storm.

"Quiet! I think I heard something."

" 'Eard something!" scoffed Smithers. "Can't 'ear meself think."

But there *was* something. From the far distance came the faint sound of a dog barking.

"*Rusty!*"

Another shout, another whistle and the dog came bounding towards his master, his shaggy coat bedraggled with rain.

"Good boy," said Hamish, bending to pat him. "Where's Miss Annabelle?"

The dog, understanding, looked up at him and held out a paw. "He wants us to follow him," said Hamish. "Go on, Rusty. Show us where she is."

It was the dog who was now leading the expedition. "This way!" he seemed to say, turning tail and darting off up the hillside with the others scrambling at his tail, wondering how Annabelle could have followed such a difficult trail.

"He's making for Old Morag's cottage!" cried Macpherson in amazement. "How on earth could she have got there?"

He could not believe his eyes. But there she was, sitting safe and sound in an old easy-chair, with the cocks and hens clucking around her and the cat snuggling quietly in her arms. Old Morag was rocking herself around the kitchen, bringing out cups from the cupboard, trying to make a meal for herself and her guest.

"Mercy me!" said Macpherson, greatly relieved. "How did you get here?"

"It was a miracle." Annabelle's eyes were shining as if she had just seen a vision. "You'll never believe it, Macpherson."

" 'E'll believe anything, Miss Hannabelle." Smithers was shaking himself at the door before entering. "I ain't 'alf glad to see you're hokay."

"But *how*?" Macpherson wanted to know about the miracle. "Tell me, Annabelle."

Annabelle told him. "I was sitting there on the heather after you left me when suddenly I seemed to hear a voice . . ."

The old woman rocked towards her, nodding her head. "A voice!" she quavered.

"That's right. I was warning you about the danger from the sky."

"But how could she hear from that distance?" puzzled Macpherson.

"And who would be explaining a miracle?" said Old Morag sharply. "There are things none of us understand. None of us!"

Macpherson felt a strange shivery feeling at his spine. He had often imagined miracles, and here he was learning about a real one.

"The voice seemed to come from nowhere, and yet from everywhere," went on Annabelle. "Rusty heard it, too. You should have seen him pricking up his ears. I felt I *had* to obey it, though I knew I would not be able to walk. 'Come up to the cottage', it said. 'Up to the cottage'."

"Jings! What did you do?"

"Just as I got to my feet the storm started. I was so afraid that I tried to run, but my ankle gave way and I fell down. Then *she* came and helped me."

"She?" Macpherson's eyes were wide with suspense.

"The White Lady," said Annabelle in a faraway voice.

"Blimey!" cried Smithers, turning white himself.

"You mean, the ghost!" cried Macpherson.

"I knew you wouldn't believe me," said Annabelle. "Yes, it was the ghost. Truly. I didn't imagine it. She just appeared there in front of me and helped me up the hill. She carried me over the rough bits. Oh! how gentle her arms were and how strong. I can't explain how it happened, but all of a sudden I was here. And the White Lady was gone."

Macpherson was too dumbfounded to speak. Was it true? Yet, why should Annabelle make up such a story, and how else could she have reached the cottage?

True or false, what did it matter as long as she was safe and they were all under the shelter of Old Morag's roof.

Big Hamish had come forward and was clasping Morag's twisted old hand. "So it's yourself, Hamish?" She looked up at him with tears in her eyes. "It's many a long day since you've been here. Not since the lad . . ."

"I'm here now." Hamish patted her shoulder. "And thanks to you, or somebody, Miss Annabelle's safe. Wait now, and I'll get a fire going so that we can all dry ourselves and have a hot cup of tea."

It was a strange but happy party that took place in the higgledy-piggledy kitchen. Shared by the cocks and hens and the lean cat. And with the storm still raging overhead.

Everyone helped. Big Hamish lit the fire and set the kettle on to boil. Macpherson opened out the parcels of food they had brought with them. Annabelle buttered the scones. Old Morag set the dishes on the table. Even Smithers did his share, seizing the old broomstick and sweeping up the kitchen, chasing the cackling fowls out of his way.

At last they all sat round the fire with cups of steaming hot tea in their hands, listening to the dying rumble of the thunder and to Old Morag's tales. It was so long since she had had anyone to talk to. So long since she had seen such a bright fire. So long since she had tasted good food.

"You'll come again?" she said when it was all over and they were preparing to go. "You won't forget?" She looked appealingly at Big Hamish, wrapping Annabelle in a rug ready to carry her home to the castle.

"Ay, we'll come," he promised in such a voice that Old Morag knew he would keep his word.

It was not only Hamish who kept his word. In the week that followed there was never a

day when the creaking gate did not open and Old Morag come rocking to the door to greet a welcome visitor.

Smithers, in spite of his dislike of climbing, came with fruit and vegetables from the castle garden. Annabelle sent clothes and promises of visits when her ankle was strong enough. Big Hamish arrived with hammer and nails to tackle the running repairs. And Macpherson never failed to put in an appearance, carrying messages for her and asking, "Is there anything I can do for you, Morag?"

"Yes," she would say, welcoming him more than the others. "Sit down, Macpherson, and give me your company."

That was what she wanted most of all. Company. Someone to listen to. Someone who would listen to her. Macpherson sat on a little stool at her feet and told her everything, in the same way he told Grandpa. All about the great big bird that lived high on the mountain. About how he was going to compete in the Highland Games. About his almost-forgotten life as a message-boy in the far-off city of Glasgow.

That was what Old Morag liked to hear best. She had never been out of the glen in her life and could not imagine what it must be like to live amongst crowds. Macpherson did his best to paint a true picture for her of skyscrapers, of the ship-building yards on the great river Clyde, of Old Skinflint's shop and of the traffic in the busy streets.

He told her about the Highland bobby and about wee Maisie Murphy who always called him Macpherthon.

In turn she told him of sights she had seen even stranger than those in Glasgow. Sights which only she could see. Macpherson was a good listener. He sat quietly, taking it all in, so that he could retell it to Grandpa when he got home. It would take days to tell him everything.

Macpherson wondered if he should ask her about the future, if she could foresee who was to win the Hundred Yards for Youths at the Highland Games. But maybe it would be better not to know.

"I'll tell you this much," said the old woman, reading his thoughts. "You'll hear a Voice."

"Mercy me!" Macpherson looked startled. What did she mean? Would it be her Voice? Or the White Lady's?

"Wait and see," was all Old Morag would tell him.

8

Treasure Island

"Steady on, Macpherson! Watch out for the rocks. A little bit to the left. That's the ticket."

Macpherson, hand on the tiller, obeyed Big Hamish's instructions, guiding the boat carefully past the rocks, setting course for one of the small islands in the distance.

It was the biggest and greenest of the little group dotted about in the waters around Glen Bogle.

"Ay, that's the one. There's enough good grass there for sheep to feed on," said Hamish with satisfaction. "Carry on, Macpherson."

Macpherson, Admiral of the Fleet, sailed on. They were carrying a strange cargo on board. Half a dozen sheep who were being ferried across to a fresh grazing-ground. It was another new adventure for Macpherson. Jings! He was fairly seeing life.

He had posted a card to Grandpa with a view of Glen Bogle on one side and a carefully-written greeting on the other.

How are you? I'm fine. Competing in the Highland Games on Saturday. Wish you were here. Cheerio, Macpherson. PS Tell Maisie . . .

But there was no room on the postcard to tell Maisie anything. It would just have to wait. All the same, he did wish Grandpa was here, and Maisie, too. It would make the holiday complete. In one way he wished he could follow the postcard home. In another he wished his Highland holiday would last for ever and ever.

There was never a dull moment. Fancy! Instead of trailing round the streets with a message-basket, here he was sailing away to a desert island with a cargo of sheep.

"What's it called?" he asked Big Hamish.

"The island? Och! It's too small to have a name."

"What a shame!" said Macpherson. Surely everything ought to have a name, even such a tiny island. "Could we not call it something?"

"Something Island?" Hamish gave a wide grin of amusement. "Why not Macpherson Island?"

The boy considered the matter. It would be a grand thing to have an island called after him. They might even put it on the map.

Macpherson Island. And then he had a better idea.

"Treasure Island," he suggested.

"What?" Hamish let out one of his big booming laughs. "Man, Macpherson, you've got a great imagination."

"Ay, I have."

"There's no treasure within a thousand miles of Glen Bogle. Still, if that's what you want."

"Yes, that's what I want," said Macpherson, his mind firmly made up.

"Right you are. Treasure Island it is! Steady on! A wee bit to the right. Now then, straight ahead."

With Hamish's help he edged the boat in towards the shore and held it steady while the big man stepped out and fastened the rope to a jutting-out piece of rock. The sheep, huddled together in the bottom of the boat, were loth to leave.

"Silly things!" said Macpherson, trying to heave them on to their feet. In the end Big Hamish had to carry them in his great arms, one by one, and dump them down on their new grazing-ground. At once they began to wander away as if they had lived there all their lives, chewing the fresh grass with great satisfaction.

"Ay, they'll come on fine here," said Hamish, watching them. "Are you wanting to explore for treasure, Macpherson?"

"Yes, I am," said Macpherson, stepping ashore. "Are you coming, Mr Hamish, sir?"

"Not me. I'll sit here and smoke my pipe."

Macpherson went off alone, feeling like Robinson Crusoe. There was not much to see on the island. Some stunted rowan trees and a profusion of wild flowers growing in the long grass. Macpherson picked a bunch as he went along, thinking he might take them to Old Morag. Then he wandered down to the shore to gather sea-shells.

His hands were full as he rounded a corner and came across the cave. *This* was something that must be explored. Treasure Island! Perhaps the cave was full of riches, hidden there from a pirate ship.

Macpherson could see it in his mind's eye. A chest full of pearls and rubies and diamonds. Enough to keep Grandpa in comfort for the rest of his days. He would buy him a big house by the seaside and a big yacht to sail in. And the best washing-machine in the world for Aunt Janet. As for Maisie Murphy, she would have a new outfit for every day in the week and never again have to wear borrowed garments. All he had to do was go into the cave and find the treasure.

He laid down his handful of flowers and shells and took his first step inside. It was so dark that he could not see treasure-chests or anything else. The ground was all slimy and slippery. What if there were snakes lurking there? Or wild beasts? Or a desperate criminal hiding from justice?

Macpherson blinked his eyes, wishing he could see in the dark, like Annabelle's Tiger-Cat. He would have to feel his way in. Not too far in case the cave swallowed him up. But just a few steps, enough to get really inside, and maybe he would stumble on the treasure.

He stumbled all right but not on the treasure. His feet slithered from under him and down he came on hands and knees on the damp slimy floor.

"Mercy! What a mess I'll be in," he thought, trying to raise himself up. And just then he heard a sudden strange sound. *Sniff-snuffle!* What was that? Something breathing in a dark corner. Snuffling and grunting. A desperate criminal? Or a wild beast?

Macpherson did not wait to see. Never mind the treasure. All he wanted was to get out of the cave alive and hurry back to Big Hamish.

But every time he tried to get up, his feet slithered from under him.

"Oh jings!" he gasped, backing away on his hands and knees as the grunting and snuffling came closer. Whoever was in the cave seemed to be stalking him in the darkness, shuffling nearer and nearer as if getting ready to pounce.

Macpherson the Great, once more reduced to the ranks of a fearty, backed out of the cave, trembling with terror. Not waiting to look back, ignoring the scattered flowers and sea-shells, he took to his heels and ran the fastest hundred yards of his life.

"Mr Hamish! Mr Hamish, sir!" he called as he ran, startling the grazing sheep and the big man who was leaning against a rock calmly smoking his pipe. "Help! There's something in the cave. I think it's a beast."

"A beast?" Big Hamish grinned, not taking him seriously. "Och well! Maybe it's the Loch Ness Monster. Would you like me to look?"

"D'you think it's safe?" Macpherson asked anxiously. "Had you not better take a stick or something?"

"I've got my two arms on me," said Big Hamish, flexing his muscles. "I'll manage fine. Come on, Macpherson."

Macpherson came on but at a safe distance. It was one thing being brave in your imagination. Not so easy when it came to the bit. He wished he had great strong arms like Hamish's.

"COME OUT!" Big Hamish was at the entrance of the cave, bending down and peering inside. "Come on now, whoever you are. QUICK MARCH!"

Macpherson held his breath waiting for — he did not know what — to emerge. How brave Hamish was, standing his ground like that. You could never call him a fearty.

"Here it comes, Macpherson."

First of all a little snout appeared and then a pair of flippers.

"Goodness gracious! It's a seal!" cried Macpherson, running forward, all his fears forgotten.

"Ay, that's what it is," said Hamish, standing back to let it wriggle out of the cave. "Away you go back into the water."

The seal gave a grunt as if answering him and went slithering forward, gathering speed as it neared the water's edge.

"Och! it's away," said Macpherson in a disappointed voice, as he saw its head bobbing about amongst the waves.

"You could bring it back," the big man told him. "Are you a good whistler, Macpherson?"

"Ay, I'm not bad."

"Whistle, then. They say seals like music. Have a shot, Macpherson."

Macpherson had a shot. He whistled *Pop Goes the Weasel* loud and clear. Then he tried one of Grandpa's sea-songs, *Ho-ro! Up she rises*. But it was *Scotland the Brave* that did the trick.

"Look, Macpherson, over by the rock."

"Jings!" gasped Macpherson. "*Three* seals. No, four! Och! There's a whole shoal coming."

"Keep whistling, Macpherson. I'm too busy smoking my pipe."

Macpherson whistled and whistled. One by one the seals began to gather until there were dozens twisting and turning in the water as if they were waltzing to the music. Some ventured as far as the beach and came wriggling up to Macpherson's feet.

"Oh my!" he cried, delighted at the sight and pleased that the power of his whistling had brought the strange little creatures out of the water. "I wish I could take one home to Grandpa. A present from Glen Bogle."

Big Hamish threw back his head and laughed at the thought. Then a sober look

came into his eyes and he said sadly, "I'm thinking the best present you can take back is yourself, Macpherson. Man, I'll fairly miss you when you're away."

"I'm not away yet."

There was still the Highland Games to come and plenty of adventures in front of him before his holiday was at an end. Meantime he had found some new friends.

"Look, Mr Hamish, sir. I'm sure that's the one that was in the cave. Och! I wish I could take it home."

He sat down on the beach whistling softly as the seal came slithering and sniffling towards him.

"They'll have you away with them, if you don't look out," laughed Big Hamish. "I'm going back to the boat. I'll give you two-three minutes more."

Left to himself Macpherson began to play with the seals, almost as if they were human beings. Almost as if he was playing with wee Maisie Murphy. She would have enjoyed watching them darting about in the water.

"MACPHERSON!"

There was a worried note in Big Hamish's voice as he gave a shout from the distance. "Come on! You'll have to give a hand to bale

113

out. The boat seems to have sprung a leak."

"Mercy!" cried Macpherson, springing to action. Here was yet another adventure. "What'll we bale out with, Mr Hamish, sir?"

"I've found an old cocoa-tin here, but *it*'s leaking, too. It'll be hard work keeping going."

Macpherson, running to the boat, saw that it was almost a quarter full of water. The seal came flapping after him, thinking it was all part of the game. "Will it sink, Mr Hamish?"

"I hope not," said Hamish grimly. "Come on, Macpherson. All hands on deck."

They rolled up their sleeves and took turns, time about, scooping out the water with their hands and with the leaking cocoa-tin. Then suddenly Macpherson remembered his shells. "See here!" he cried, picking up the biggest. "Will this help?"

"The very thing! Man, Macpherson, you're a genius."

It was much easier now that they could both bale together. Before long they could see the bottom of the boat. "We'll risk it," said Hamish, untying the rope. "Keep it up, Macpherson, and hope for the best."

It was like fighting a battle against the rising sea. Macpherson's arms were aching and his back was stiff, though he tried not to show it.

As fast as he scooped out one shellful, another gush of water came in through the leak at the bottom of the boat. Meantime Hamish was busy getting the engine going, and soon they were puttering away from the shore.

Macpherson had time only to give a quick look back, to shout "Cheerio!" to Treasure Island and to the seal that was trying to keep up with them. Then he bent once more to his task, baling out as hard as he could. "Keep it up, Macpherson."

The boat gathered speed. The bobbing seal was left far behind, and now the water was coming in faster. Big Hamish set to work with the cocoa-tin. In-out! In-out! But still the water was rising. "Keep going, Macpherson."

Macpherson kept going. He had no feeling in his arms. He was working blindly, bending and dipping, dipping and bending. In-out! In-out! Would it never end?

The boat was getting lower in the water. "Well done, Macpherson. We're nearly there."

Nearly there! Yes, Macpherson had a sudden sight of a whitewashed cottage and of Rusty waiting on the shore to welcome them.

They had made it!

9

The Highland Games

This was it! The great day of the Highland Games had arrived.

What a stir there was in Glen Bogle. Even the sea-birds seemed excited, screaming to each other as they circled over the field where the Games were to be held. The bolder ones settled on the grandstand where Sir George and his friends would sit, as if they, too, wanted the best view. And the boldest of them all flew up and perched on top of the flag-pole where the Scottish lion was proudly dancing in the breeze.

It was a perfect day. Not a cloud in the sky. Not a shadow on the sun. Scarcely a ripple on the sea. A day when it was wonderful to be alive. A day when all worries were forgotten. A day to be given up to enjoyment.

There was only one small niggling doubt at the back of Macpherson's mind as he stood in the cottage kitchen dressed in his new kilt. Would he be able to win the race and justify

Big Hamish's faith in him?

"Ay, of course you'll win," said Hamish, flexing his muscles for his own trial of strength. "You'll beat the lot, Macpherson. There's only Jock and Wull and Tam. Big fellas, right enough, but slow."

Macpherson was not so sure. He had watched Jock and Wull and Tam racing against each other in the field. Putting in practice as he had done himself. Big fellas all right with brawny arms and sturdy legs. They looked more like men than youths.

"Ay! You'll do, Macpherson."

Big Hamish had that strange look in his eyes and that husky tone in his voice. Macpherson knew what he was thinking.

"Did *he* . . .?" he began, looking at the picture on the mantelpiece.

Hamish nodded. "Ay, he did. Came in first. Beat the lot. It was the year before . . ."

The big man turned away, not wanting to finish the sentence; but Macpherson understood. Now, more than ever, he wanted to win. Not only for Big Hamish's sake, but for Angus's.

"I'll try my best," he promised, bracing himself and looking the lad in the picture square in the face. He had a feeling that Angus would be watching and willing him to win. Annabelle, too, sitting in the grandstand with her uncle. Though she was still limping, she was determined not to miss the Games. Especially as Macpherson was competing. He must prove himself in front of them all.

The crowds were beginning to gather at the field. Buses and cars were arriving with loads of spectators. Where in the world had they all come from? Glen Bogle, usually such a quiet place, was now stirring with people, as if it was the capital of Scotland.

Already the skirl of the bagpipes could be heard, for the piping contest was under way. In the centre of the field the judges and officials were assembling, each with a special job to do. Most important of all was the man with the gun. The starter, wearing a white coat and looking very official. He was the one who would set all the races in motion, including the highlight of Macpherson's day. The Hundred Yards for Youths.

He walked towards the tent marked COMPETITORS. It was crowded with pole-vaulters, shot-putters, hammer-throwers and big giants who were to pit their strength against Hamish at tossing the caber. Jock and Wull and Tam were there, having a snigger at

119

him behind their hands.

"See that wee fella! Could you credit it? *He*'s running against us."

"Away! He should be in his pram."

Macpherson's hackles rose. In his pram! Wait till he showed them! He walked out of the tent with his head held so high that he tripped over one of the tent-pegs and fell flat on his face.

"He-haw! He-haw!" roared the big boys, delighted at his downfall. "Look at him. He can't even walk, let alone run."

Macpherson picked himself up, flushed with shame. He hoped Sir George's party had not yet arrived and seen him tumble. But no! Wasn't it like the thing? There they were taking their places on the grandstand, looking around to see what was going on. They waved in sympathy to him as he dusted himself down. "Poor soul!" he could almost hear them saying.

If there was one thing Macpherson hated it was being pitied. He would show them who was a poor soul. He strutted off, swinging his kilt, trying to make himself look twice his size. Then suddenly he remembered Grandpa's wise words. "Pride comes before a fall." Better not swagger too soon.

He waved back at the grandstand, admiring Sir George. What a fine upstanding figure he was in the Royal Stuart tartan, with Annabelle by his side as neat as ninepence in her tartan skirt and green jacket. There were several lords and ladies around them, but it was Sir George, chieftain of the clan, who stood out above them all.

Ta-ra-ra-Ra-Ra-ra-ra!

Scotland the Brave!

They were playing the same tune he had heard in the Glasgow streets, a tune that stirred the blood and made Macpherson eager to do brave deeds for the sake of his country. Never mind the race. He could climb the highest mountain, fight the fiercest dragon, endure any danger with such a tune ringing in his ears. Macpherson the Brave!

They were marching round the field. All the different pipers and clans and competitors. Macpherson set off, too, the smallest of the lot, with a heart bigger than any.

Ta-ra-ra-RA-RA-ra-ra!

He saluted Sir George as he passed, receiving a special smile from him and a wave from Annabelle's little gloved hand. Though he was at the end of the procession he pretended he was leading it.

"Forward, men! Follow your leader! Into battle!"

And now the important man in the white coat was looking down the muzzle of his gun. The judges were marking the ground where the shot-putters had pitched their throws, and Big Hamish was taking off his jacket ready to toss the great caber.

"The best of luck, Mr Hamish, sir," said Macpherson, running towards him and wishing he had such fine muscles.

"Thanks, Macpherson. Stand back."

Big Hamish spat on his hands. The crowd held their breath. The Highland dancers twirled in vain. All attention was riveted on the big man.

Hamish bent down and lifted the heavy pole, staggering a little under its weight. The crowd gasped. Would he drop it before he could toss it from him so that it fell in the proper way, head-over-tail? No! Not Big Hamish. He found his balance and ran forward a few steps carrying the caber between his hands. Imagine carrying a monster of a telegraph-pole like that! Then suddenly he gave a grunt and tossed it from him.

A cheer from the crowd. Big Hamish had done it. It was a record toss.

"Oh my! I'm awful proud of you, Mr Hamish, sir," cried Macpherson, rushing to congratulate him.

He held out his hand and tried not to wince when Hamish grasped it in his. "Thanks, Macpherson. Now it's your turn."

His big moment had come.

Macpherson took off his jacket, wishing his arms were not so puny. Even with all the porridge he had eaten, he was still skinny. Never mind; he would do his best.

Jock and Wull and Tam were lining up on their marks, still sniggering at the thought of running against such an insignificant little nobody. It was a good laugh, if nothing else.

"Come on, the wee fella! Where's your pram?"

Macpherson tried not to listen to them. He was watching the man in the white coat, waiting for him to shout: "On your marks! Get set!" before firing off his gun. A good start was half the battle, but Macpherson knew he would need more than that. Some inspiration to spur him on to the winning-post.

Then he recalled Old Morag's words. "You'll hear a Voice."

He raised his head hopefully and listened. Whose voice would it be? Old Morag's? The

White Lady's? Or . . .?

There it was! "*Come away, Macpherson!*"

It was Grandpa's voice as plain as anything. Grandpa, cheering him all the way from Glasgow.

There it was again, but with a difference. "*Come away, Mac-pher-thon!*" Maisie Murphy. Fancy hearing her!

Another voice. "*Come away, Macpherson!*" Goodness gracious! It was the Highland bobby's.

"*Ho-ro! Up she rises!*"

It was Grandpa's once more, sounding so like himself that Macpherson looked round in the direction of the grandstand. Jings! They were there in real life, the three of them, sitting in the stand waving like mad in his direction.

"*Come away, Macpherson!*"

Macpherson was too bamboozled to wonder how it had happened. All he could see was Grandpa's white beard, the feather nodding in Maisie's borrowed hat, and the Highland bobby looking unlike himself in a plain tweed suit. Jings! Fancy them coming all the way from Glasgow just to see *him*.

"On your marks! Get set!"

Macpherson was set at the first shout. He had something to run for now, with Grandpa and wee Maisie Murphy and the Highland bobby cheering him on. The man in the white coat raised his pistol high in the air.

Crack!

Macpherson shot off as if he had been fired from the pistol. His feet went flying, hardly taking time to reach the ground. "*Come away, Macpherson!*" It was not only Grandpa and Maisie and the Highland bobby who were shouting. Not only Sir George and Annabelle and Smithers. The whole crowd seemed to be cheering him on. "*Come away, Macpherson!*" And somewhere in the midst of it all he heard a big booming voice shouting, "*Come away, Angus!*" It was Big Hamish, carried away by the occasion, forgetting that the boy in the kilt was not his own lost son.

But it was Grandpa's voice that did the trick. It was his "*Come away, Macpherson!*" that won the day. How could Macpherson help winning when he knew the old man was watching? The tape was in front of him. Another two-three steps and he would break through. He had done it! He was first!

Jock and Wull and Tam came lumbering after him, puffing and panting, but with the grace to shake him by the hand and say, "Well done, the wee fella!"

A great cheer from the crowd. "*Well done, Macpherson!*" Grandpa rose to his feet and waved his arms in the air, while wee Maisie Murphy's feather bounced up and down with excitement. "*Well done, Macpherthon!*" Well done, indeed!

Big Hamish gave him such a pat on the back that he almost knocked him to the ground. "Man, Macpherson, I knew you'd do it. Shake!" Again Macpherson tried not to wince with pain as his hand was swallowed up in the big man's.

"Thanks, Mr Hamish, sir. It was your training that did it."

Macpherson did his best to look modest

when it came to the presenting of the prizes. He put on his jacket, slicked down his tousled hair and marched up with the others to the front of the grandstand where Sir George was doing the honours.

He had a good view of Grandpa now — they could exchange nods and winks — and of wee Maisie sucking away at a lollipop and beaming brightly at her hero. The Highland bobby gave him a thumbs-up salute, and Annabelle clapped her little gloved hands. It was great!

"First prize for the Hundred Yards for Youths. Macpherson."

The crowd cheered and clapped as the small kilted figure came forward and saluted.

"Well done, boy! Not bad for a fearty!"

Sir George's eyes were twinkling as he shook hands with Macpherson and handed him a small cup along with an envelope containing money.

"Thank you, Sir George, sir."

Macpherson stepped back and raised the cup so that Grandpa could see. How much money was in the envelope? Enough, he hoped, to buy presents for everyone. If not big things, at least "little mindings" for Grandpa and Maisie and Annabelle and Old Morag and Big Hamish.

As for himself he needed no mindings. As long as he lived he would never forget his Highland holiday in Glen Bogle or the sound of Grandpa's shaky old voice cheering him on.

"Come away, Macpherson!"